KENNA CHARLES

Beyond Touch

D1739178

First edition

Editing by Briggs Consulting

This book was professionally typeset on Reedsy.
Find out more at reedsy.com

For Nigel, who has my whole heart.

Contents

Chapter One

Thursday

"Grocery store shelves have been picked clean today as residents of the Portland Metro Area prepare for the upcoming storm. City officials are advising residents to have candles or battery operated lights on hand, and to make sure warm clothing and blankets are available, as the power will almost certainly be turned off as a preventative measure against fires from lightning strikes." The news anchor stared into the camera, seemingly trying to remain interested in the third day of reporting about a storm on its way. "Climate and fire experts agree that our atypically dry weather has created a greater than normal risk of wildfires due to lightning strikes. Heavy rain is expected to follow the initial lightning event. The storm is expected within the hour."

"Lorna! Do we have enough food?" Kahrren tried to shout to her best friend and roommate who was behind the bathroom door, preparing for a romantic evening with her boyfriend. Kahrren's voice was just above a loud, gravelly whisper, despite her best effort to push herself into normal sounding speech.

"What?" A plume of steam poured from the hallway bathroom as she opened the door. Lorna insisted Kahrren should have the master bedroom with ensuite bathroom while she "convalesced."

"Do we have enough food? The news is reporting how shelves have been

1

picked clean."

"Yes, we are fine. I shopped this morning and Andrew is bringing over even more groceries, even though I told him we didn't need them. And knowing him, he will order a bunch of takeout too." She removed the towel from her hair and used it to wipe the mirror, and clicked her tongue when it only removed the surface moisture and not the underlying fogginess.

Kahrren waved her hand rapidly through the air in an attempt to mitigate the steam's effect on her hair. Sadly, there was too much moisture coming from the rainforest level humidity of Lorna's bathroom for it to be helped.

"Sorry. Too late. You're frizzy." Lorna quirked one side of her mouth apologetically as she stepped out of the bathroom and crossed the hall to her bedroom, clad in only a towel.

"Perfect." Kahrren walked back to her own bathroom and tried to tame the flyaway condition of her once smooth hair. She combed and sprayed for a few minutes, but the problem only seemed to get worse. She heaved a sigh and tossed the comb on the counter and turned to exit the bathroom.

"Hiiiiiieeeeeeeeee, Kaaaahreeeen! Did you miss me?"

"Didn't even notice you were gone."

"Rude! Aren't you supposed to be, like, nice to me now since you got me killed? Seems like the least you could do."

"Sorry, Brittany. You're right. I should be nice to you. But to be fair, you popped up on me when I was attempting a dramatic exit from the bathroom due to uncooperative hair."

"Hmm. You're right. Your hair is doing a little something right..." She pointed to the side of Kahrren's head, making a disapproving face. She said, "Ooh, girl, no."

"Move or I'll walk through you."

"You *know* I don't like that!"

"Sure do. Now step aside. Someone's at the door."

"It's Andrew. He has a lot of bags."

"Then *move* so I can help him! You pest."

The sweet, heart-shaped face of the young dead woman contorted, dropping her jaw and wrinkling her nose as she stepped out of the way.

There was a firm knocking on the front door and Kahrren hobbled has quickly as she could to allow boyfriend ingress. "Come on in, Andrew."

"Thanks. I come bearing provisions." His arms lifted slightly, illustrating the burden of many bags.

"Whoa. What's in here?" she asked, taking as many of the bags as she could manage.

"A little bit of everything, really. I wanted to make sure you guys have what you need."

"That we *all* have what we need," Lorna corrected as she stepped into the entryway and took Kahrren's load, plus a couple of bags from Andrew. "You shouldn't be carrying heavy stuff, Kahrren." She set the bags on the kitchen counter, then took the remainder of what Andrew carried and placed the bags next to the others. "Now go sit down." Her finger firmly pointed to the living room, paired perfectly with a stern face.

"We've got it, Kahrren. Go sit. Before Lorna has a conniption fit." He dug through one of the bags and pulled out a bottle of juice, handing it to the perceived invalid as she gave up the fight and retreated.

Andrew slid his arm around Lorna's waist and pressed a sweet, if loud, kiss on her lips. Kahrren made a gagging noise and headed for the living room, passing the sneering specter who was a constant, and frankly, unwelcome presence since her death several months earlier.

"This should get us through a few days," Andrew said to Lorna as he started putting away the groceries. "Plus, there's a bunch of stuff on the way from a few restaurants."

"Thank you, but you didn't have to do that."

"Well, we have to eat. Since I am hunkering down here for the storm, I wanted to make sure I didn't eat everything you have."

"I know. I don't want to leave Kahrren yet. Especially if something happens and I can't get to her."

"I agree. It's a good idea for us all to be together." Kahrren saw him peek out of the kitchen at her. Though he noticeably lowered the volume of his speech, she heard him. "And since she won't come to my place, we'll make it work here."

"Thank you," she said softly.

Kahrren ambled to the couch and gingerly leaned back to sit. Though more than five months had passed since nearly losing her life at the hands of a killer, she'd been so badly beaten the fact that she was even alive was nothing short of a miracle. As a result of the event, her movements were slow and labored due to severe and constant pain.

"In local news tonight, we have learned the convicted child molester, Enoch Keres, was released from prison earlier this month after serving a sentence of twenty-five years for the kidnapping and sexual assault of the child known as 'The Boy in the Barn.'" Kahrren sat up and turned to the television, rapt.

* * *

Monday

"Hey, kid. Time to get the show on the road."

Mitch looked at his older partner inquisitively. "I guess criminals don't take breaks because of storms."

"Guess not. But we're headed somewhere I've never been before."

"And what fresh hell awaits us today?"

"A museum."

"Huh?"

Jim Sharp shrugged his shoulders. "One of those dead body exhibits."

"Oh. Like the preserved bodies? Those are actually kind of cool. But you *have* been to a museum before, right?"

"Of course I have. But not in a very long time." Sharp held up his keys and shook them, indicating it was time to go.

"All right, just let me get—"

"Don't you dare."

"My jacket, you grump." He slid on his suit jacket and raincoat over top. "I already drank my kombucha today."

Sharp made a face as he pretended to shudder. "Yuck."

"I'll give up kombucha *and* seaweed chips if you give up smoking," Mitch challenged.

"Just don't drink that stuff around me."

They arrived at the Portland Museum of Science and exited the car through a deluge of rain. "Nice to be back to rain instead of those lightning storms," Mitch said.

"Yeah. I hate when the power is off. People lose their grip." They approached the entry of the museum, the door opening automatically. A group of police officers stood in the lobby, looking more discomposed than usual. "That ain't a good sign," he said only loud enough for Mitch to hear, then spoke up. "What've we got, sir?"

Lieutenant Marco Rodriguez turned to the arriving detectives. Usually a handsome man, his face was drawn inward and uncharacteristically ashen today. "I had to come see this one for myself. Just when you think there's nothing new under the sun..." He waved for the men to follow him as walked back into the exhibit rooms. Sharp and Adams gave each other a questioning glance and followed their boss.

There were officers and crime scene technicians all waiting at a distance for the detectives to have a chance to see the scene as it lay. Everyone in the room stared at the body, a mutilated semblance of a human shape, perfectly preserved in a massive, translucent, rectangular block.

"How in hell did it get like *that?*" Sharp had seen hundreds of dead bodies during his career, maybe even thousands. "I've never seen anything like it."

Adams stared at it, entirely at a loss as to where to begin. "Uh... a little help here, boss?"

He looked to Rodriguez and then to Sharp for ideas, but they seemed as baffled as he.

Rodriguez said to the team, "I guess get all the photos you can, then check for fingerprints on and around the plinth, and on the block, itself. We'll have to transport the body in the... plastic? What the hell is that, actually?"

One of the technicians offered, "It looks like they wanted to give the illusion of plastination without going through the process. It takes a long time to do that. So this could be resin, maybe?"

"Could be. Resin can be bought in bulk pretty easily for stuff like table tops or even jewelry," Rodriguez agreed. "He cast his eyes around the room, responding to the sea of faces staring at him. "What? My wife makes stuff with it," he clarified, defending his masculinity. "I have seen enough. I'm going back to the precinct. Sharp, you let me know if you need anything."

"Yes, sir," he acknowledged as the Lieutenant departed. He turned to the company of officers and techs. "While you get photos," he gestured to the tech holding the camera, "the rest of you check all of the other surfaces for fingerprints or fibers, any other kind of abnormality. This is gonna be a complete shit show with thousands of people in here every day." The group scattered to start collecting evidence. "Who found the body?"

"The museum curator found it this morning. She's in the lobby, pretty upset."

"Come on, kid. That's where we're heading."

* * *

"Time for physical therapy, Kahrren. I already called to make sure they're open today." Lorna's chipper attitude was undying, and unappreciated.

"Oh, goodie. Aren't you helpful."

Kahrren's tone was clearly making a rhetorical statement, not asking a question. All the same, Lorna answered, "Yep. What would you do without me?" She grinned and pushed the door open, holding out a large, lidded paper cup with a green siren on it. "You will be *rewarded*," she sang.

"Give me the coffee if you want to live."

"I will. Once you get to the living room." Carrying the drink away, Lorna retreated to the living room and placed it next to Kahrren's favorite spot to sit. She shouted down the hall, "I'll make breakfast!"

Hair still pasted to her face on one side, sticking straight up on the other, Kahrren shuffled stiffly into the living room, and made her way to her seat.

"I hope you're going to fix your hair before you go out." Brittany could be so critical for a corpse, though she seemed to be living her best unlife. Whenever she showed up she was sporting her favorite leggings and hoodie. Her hair and makeup were always perfect, if a little whitewashed due to the fact that she was now a being of light. Or some shit.

"Why are you *still here*? You've been dead for five months. What do you want from me?"

"I want to be gone as much as you want me to be. What do I know about being a ghost? You're stuck with me until one of us figures out why I'm here."

"Oh, goodie."

"What's goodie?" Lorna carried in warmed up leftovers. "Here. Your favorite."

"Thanks." She accepted the bowl of Two Cans of Anything Casserole and stirred it. "Why does this stuff reheat so unevenly? You can have a scorching hot bite and then a freezing cold bite. It's weird."

"The price you pay for the convenience of nuked food, I guess." She sat with her coffee and took back the conversation. "Who were you talking to? What did you 'oh, goodie' about?"

The pretext of the conversation was friendly curiosity. The subtext reeked of "What aren't you telling me?"

"You don't know when to quit, do you?"

"Of course I do. It's when I get what I want."

"And you say *I'm* droll."

Lorna grinned, steadfast in her commitment to find out what Kahrren didn't want to say. "You think I haven't figured out that you aren't talking to either me or yourself?"

Kahrren blinked pronouncedly from an otherwise blank face. "I'll tell you if you promise to go to Andrew's for a weekend and leave me alone."

"No." She sipped her coffee. "You'll tell me because I will nag you until you do."

"Fine." She set down her bowl and sipped her own drink. "But please don't tell Andrew. I know you already told him about my ability."

Lorna's mouth dropped and her eyes widened. "I… Well…"

"It's fine. Since he knows now, it's actually a little easier for me. And I appreciate him not asking questions about it. But he might if he knows this."

"Jeeze, what the hell, Kahrren?" Her face changed from guilty to worried.

"My abilities started getting stronger shortly before the time of the... um... incident. They went through the roof after my injuries." Taking a moment to sip her mocha, she watched her friend's face to see how she would take it. Lorna seemed steady enough, so Kahrren continued. "Now I pick up stuff without having to touch anything first. I hear or see people's thoughts as they think them. And... well... Bruce Willis is gonna come walking in any minute."

"Ummm... *What?!?*"

"I have been seeing Brittany since I woke up in the hospital."

"Are you saying *you see dead people?*"

"Yes. Amongst other things."

"You've been talking to Brittany all this time?"

Kahrren picked up her bowl and shoveled in a mouthful. "Mmmhmm."

"Are you sure you're not having hallucinations? Like from brain damage?"

Kahrren shrugged as she finished chewing and swallowed. "I have no idea. Could be. But I don't think so. Because I can hear what you're thinking before you say it. I've tested it multiple times."

"Like, actively and all the time?"

Kahrren grinned. "I wish I could 'close my eyes' when you think of stuff like that." A big fan of using air quotes, she employed them here. Lorna gasped and covered her face with both her hands, realizing she was busted for thinking of her very hot boyfriend, au naturel.

"No!"

"Yep."

"*No!*"

Talking through her chuckle, she said, "Yep." She took another bite as Lorna's mind spun into a vortex of impropriety. "I have no idea how you come off as so sweet with the filth going through your mind."

"Stop it!" Lorna jumped up off of the chair, grabbed her coffee and escaped to the kitchen, to the sound of Kahrren's exaggerated laughing.

"Well, that was kinda fun." Brittany grinned at Kahrren, clearly having enjoyed the little display.

"Mmmhmm. You're welcome." She grinned back at the ghost of the girl. "I waited for you to be around to do that, you know. So I could be nice to you."

"Thank you. I do appreciate that." She moved toward the door. "I'll disappear for a while so you can take a shower in peace."

"See ya later." She sat in the living room and drank her coffee quietly, allowing Lorna a bit of perceived privacy to collect herself.

Chapter Two

Still Monday

Cindy and Mason were waiting for Kahrren's arrival at Thrive. The co-op where she worked was populated by all top-notch professionals, and her massage colleagues were more than great therapists, they were great friends. To show their support for her recovery, they made a point to await her arrival in the lobby every time she was scheduled. They met her three times per week with a group hug. Since Kahrren's increase in abilities, touching really didn't matter anymore, so she welcomed the physical contact, especially by such wonderful human beings.

"How are you feeling today?" Mason greeted her.

"Oh, you know… living the dream." In illustration, she raised the cane with which she had been forced to walk when she was outside of the house. A few steps on carpet she could manage on her own, but not more than that.

"Are you ready for massage yet?" Cindy was eager to be a part of Kahrren's recovery.

"Yes. I got the go ahead from my doctor last week, so I'll schedule before I leave today. We will have to be very gentle though. Everything still hurts."

Cindy pulled Kahrren into another hug. "Of course, my friend. I've got your back."

"Me too. Anytime you need." Mason kissed the top of her head in a friendly and affectionate manner then headed back into the quiet space where the private treatment rooms were. Cindy accompanied Kahrren to the physical therapy gym, leaving her in the competent hands of one of the PT Aides.

An agonizing two hours later, Lorna returned to retrieve Kahrren, who was hobbling out of the PT gym, feeling a little worse for wear. "You ready?" she asked.

"I have to stop at the front desk. Can you help me?"

Since Kahrren *never* asked for help this way, Lorna dashed to her side. "Are you okay?"

Wincing, she replied, "He put me through it a bit today. I am definitely feeling it." She made it to the reception area and leaned on the countertop. "I'll be okay. We agreed I needed to kick it up a notch if I ever want to get better."

"Hi, Kahrren. What can I do for you today?" The new receptionist was phenomenal. Mellow without being lazy, competent, and pleasant to be around, she had the place running like clockwork.

"Hi, Julie. I want to double check my PT appointments for the next few weeks and add massage on Mondays and Fridays with either Cindy or Mason. I don't know the new woman, so I'd prefer to stay with them if it's possible."

"Absolutely." A few clicks later she confirmed, "You're all set. Here is your treatment schedule, and last week you asked for your bill, so that's also in there." She folded the schedule and placed it in an envelope, with a warm but knowing smile.

Kahrren noticed the mildly weird face Julie made but said nothing. There was so much swimming through her head, she couldn't pick anything out to define the look. "Thanks very much. I'll see you Wednesday."

With Lorna's assistance they made it down the hall, taking a short break on the bench outside the elevator. After a few minutes Kahrren rose and pressed the elevator button. "Okay. Let's go." The pair walked into the elevator. Lorna pushed the button for the first floor as Kahrren stated, "I have a very important question."

Lorna's face twisted and her eyes bulged. She asked, "What is it?" She clutched nervously at her throat.

"Since I have to go to work with you so you can babysit me, do you think

Andrew will feed me?"

Lorna playfully air-smacked Kahrren near the upper arm. "You *jerk!*" Placing her hand on her forehead to calm herself, she said, "I thought you were freaking serious!"

"I am serious! I'm starving!" She grinned. "But really, I need to take pain meds today, so I have to eat. Can we get something?"

"Yes. He is already taking care of it."

"You are so lucky to have each other. I am so glad you guys finally got together." The comment was a little out of Kahrren's norm, but seemed to be appreciated by her best friend. "But if you think I am wearing the hideous dress you circled in whatever bridal magazine you were looking at while you were waiting for me in the car, you're out of your damn mind."

"Not even if it's in black?"

"Not even."

Lorna put her arm around Kahrren's ribs, stealing a quick, gentle hug. Kahrren smiled softly at the brief display of affection, one of many Lorna had recently started pausing to share with her. The two shared the embrace until the elevator doors slid open. Lorna adjusted her grip to one of support and helped Kahrren to the car.

"Now I have a question."

"Ooh, you sound serious."

"Well, it's not a serious matter but I am asking in earnest."

"I'm intrigued."

Lorna's long blonde waves bounced around her face as she shook her head, wondering why she was even asking this. "Since your abilities are, uh... stronger now, can you see the future?"

"Not so far." Kahrren grunted as she got into the car. "But who knows if that'll change. Everything else has."

Lorna helped Kahrren get belted in and closed her door. They departed the Thrive parking lot and headed for Glenn Commercial Properties where lunch was waiting.

Tuesday

Dr. Arnie Bauer faced his long-time friend, Detective Sharp, each standing on one side of the body. "I have no idea what the effects of this resin are going to be on the body. But I am afraid he'll start to decompose. I want to get him out of this as soon as possible. We have been keeping the block in cold storage to prevent any decay, as far as it's possible."

"What if you cut the resin with a saw as close as you can get it to the body, then try a chemical solvent? Is there anything that wouldn't really harm the body?"

"Any chemical will have an effect, but I am debating what will be the least harmful and weighing it against the importance of any evidence we may be able to get from the body, assuming there is any. If it hasn't already been destroyed from whatever the hell he used to get the body in this state."

"He? You know something I don't know?"

"Nah. Just assuming. Never heard of a woman doing anything like this."

"Any idea what the process would be for something like this?"

Arnie uncrossed his arms, brought his left hand up to his face, rubbed over the entire area and rested his cheek on his hand, in a thinking man's posture. "I assumed finding him in a plastination exhibit would be a good jumping off point, so I spent hours researching what it would take to turn a body into something like one of those exhibits. It seems the most time consuming part is positioning it, which doesn't seem to be an issue here. This guy is laying on his back. No real trick to it." He started walking around the resin block, describing his theory as to how the man ended up in the block. "If I am right, the body is halfway plastinated, which means bathed or soaked in formaldehyde to kill bacteria, then soaked in acetone to remove water. It would at least slow the decomp if it was done with any kind of skill. But who knows, really." He shook his head in disbelief. "The next step is forcing a chemical of some kind into the tissues of the body. Usually it's done in a vacuum and it's the most important step in plastination. But you need a lot of equipment and skill to do that. So, I'm thinking our killer skipped that step and put him in liquid resin instead. If it cures right, it hardens. Looks like he created a casing out of panes of flat resin, you know, like glass, and affixed them to create the basic formation of the block." He pointed to the inside seams of the cube. "You can see around the edges; it looks like it's sealed. I am guessing a clear silicone caulking, maybe. I think he was trying to keep the resin from leaking out the seams. Then he could mix up the resin a few gallons at a time and pour it over the body, encasing it."

Sharp actually looked impressed. "Wow. You seem like you've got a good idea of how he got this way."

"Well, I'll have a better grasp of what happened once we get him out. The resin may be stuck to the tissue, but I really won't know until I get there. The moisture and gases coming from the body are unknown factors in how the resin will react. I've never seen anything like this. I may have to resort to using acetone to get it to loosen so I can peel it away. Because most of the skin is gone, I think it'll be more likely to cause damage."

"Do you think that'll obscure the cause of death?"

"Maybe. But we may not have a choice. I'd like to be able to get *some* kind of evidence from this guy. I'm going to do some scans once I cut the block back and can fit him in the machine. Hopefully that will preserve anything I need to know. Just in case."

"Mmm-hmm." This situation being even more out of Sharp's purview than Arnie's, he really had nothing to offer or argue. "Let me know when you get somewhere with it, will ya?"

"Always do."

Sharp patted Arnie on the shoulder a couple times as a gesture of gratitude and farewell. He returned to the precinct to share his info with Adams and Rodriguez.

* * *

14

Adams was perched on the corner of his desk, tidily dressed, every hair in place. Rodriguez stood facing him, arms akimbo, taking in everything the young detective had to offer. "She didn't know anything. She was so shaken we couldn't get much out of her at first. Once she calmed down all she said was she saw the block with the body and called 9-1-1. She waited outside until someone showed up."

"Hey, Sharp. Did Dr. Bauer have any info?" He turned his body slightly, dividing his attention to include both men.

"He thinks the guy did a kind of DIY plastination." He set down the bags of lunch he'd picked up on the way back on Adams' desk and started unpacking them as he explained Arnie's theory. "Real plastination requires a bunch of expensive equipment and some real skill. So, he thinks this guy got soaked in a bunch of chemicals then put in regular resin, skipping the hard stuff." He handed Adams a salad, pulling out a chicken sandwich for himself and one for Rodriguez.

"Thanks." Rodriguez accepted the sandwich and went straight back to business as he unwrapped it. "Did he say when he thought he'd have more information?"

"Unfortunately there are too many variables, so he isn't sure. But he is actively working on it." Sharp explained Arnie's plan to extract the body, as well as the potential roadblocks he faced. Though to an average person such lunchtime conversation would be taboo, when bodies were your business, there was no room for weak stomachs.

"I got in touch with the lab manager and asked him to prioritize all evidence collected from the scene. They collected a massive number of samples. Most of them aren't going to be relevant, but at this point it's our best bet until we hear back from Bauer." Rodriguez turned and started toward his office. "Let me know if you think of any other angles to follow. For now, catch up on other reports you've been lagging on."

"Yes, sir." Adams placed himself in his chair as Sharp collected the rest of his lunch and plunked down at his desk. "Thanks for lunch, Jim."

"Mmhmm. Don't make a thing out of it. I was hungry."

"You could *try you're welcome*, you know. I'm just saying."

"Shaddup." He grinned at the kid playfully. Adams returned his smile and the team caught up on reports, declarations, and various other types of paperwork. The time was almost a gift.

"Almost seems quiet without chasing something down, doesn't it?"

"Oh, come on, kid. What did ya go and say something like that for?"

"What do you mean? *You* don't believe in superstitions," he said almost tauntingly. "Are you afraid saying how quiet it is will be some kind of cosmic challenge for things to go sideways?"

"It'll be your fault when it does."

Chapter Three

"Honey, I'm home," Andrew whispered as he entered Lorna's place and saw her rapidly waving arms and overexaggerated hand gestures indicating a balled up massage therapist on the couch. He made a sad face in commentary to how miserable she looked. Kahrren exhibited none of the peace an average sleeping person would.

Lorna whispered back, "Hi. Long time no see." She crossed the room to give him a smooch, and took his hand, leading him into the kitchen. "She fell asleep a little while ago. She was trying to hide it from me, but she kept wiping at her eyes. She is in a lot of pain."

"That sucks. She shouldn't have worked so hard yesterday."

"I agree but she didn't want to hear about it. She is entirely focused on getting better."

"Who could blame her?" Lorna poured them each a mug of tea, then they sat at the kitchen table. "I tried to pay her bill at Thrive, but they said it was paid in full. Any idea who would have done it?"

"They told me the same thing. And Kahrren was pissed off when she saw the 'Paid In Full' mark on the bill they gave her yesterday. She accused me of paying it. When I insisted it wasn't me, she demanded to know whether it was you."

"Wasn't me. Who else is there?"

"I couldn't say but I wonder if it was Beth, or *his* wife. Since she is the owner of the business, after all."

"I don't think it would be out of line for the wife of her attacker to want to make things right, do you?"

"I think it's the least she can do considering what happened. Now that Susan Martin *knows* she owns the business I think she is trying to be helpful. She can definitely afford it now since she has Beth running the business. But Kahrren doesn't want anything from her."

"Really?"

"Mmmhmm." Lorna took a moment to sip at her drink. "Mmmm. Good," she said, before returning to her explanation. "Turns out all the business documents were in Susan Martin's name. Beth told me Susan said she didn't sign them, but since they put the holding in her name, she wasn't going to dispute them either."

"I never suspected Derek Martin was so damn shady. He really pulled it over on *everyone*."

"You're not kidding. The only one he didn't fool is the one who is suffering the most."

"Asshole." Andrew was still very angry at the man he had thought was his friend. They sat for a few moments in contemplative silence before carrying on. "I don't think I'll ever get over him trying to frame me for murder. It still makes me sick."

"I know. I am so glad it's over. It'll go back to being a reputable company. Beth is doing a great job putting that place back together. She is running all the crews and everything. She isn't the owner, but she is totally the boss. Susan Martin is the boss on paper, but it's Beth's show now."

"Which is a good thing?"

"Yes. It's exactly the type of work Beth excels at. Also, it means we will have more opportunities for networking."

"Well, I don't hate that."

"I didn't think you would." She smiled sweetly at her beau.

"Ew. Gross. Nobody wants to wake up to that." Kahrren hobbled into the kitchen, in poorly enough shape she'd reverted to using her walker.

"Well, well, well, Granny. How's it going?" Andrew and Kahrren had developed such a good relationship in the time since her devastating attack.

"Hey, Daddy Warbucks. Having a bit of a rough one today. Do I smell dinner?"

"No, but sit. I'll make you something." Lorna jumped up and pulled out a chair for her infirm friend.

"Thanks." She groaned and winced down into the chair. "I really appreciate you guys taking care of me." She smiled at Andrew, becoming weepy as she did.

"God, what's wrong?" Andrew jumped up and rushed to Kahrren's side as Lorna tried to wave him off, disregarded.

"I'm okay. When I feel this rotten I get weepy." She waved him away with two quick strokes through the air. He understood he was effectively dismissed.

"Okay. Sorry. I don't want to smother you. It's hard seeing you like this."

"Don't worry your pretty little face," she said to him, trying to smirk. "I plan on taking more medication after I eat, and I'll disappear for the evening. You won't have to see me for long."

"You really are jaded, you know that?" He grinned at Kahrren as her plate was set in front of her.

Scooping up a large hunk of leftover enchilada, she mumbled, "Mmmhmm," around the bite. Finishing, she asked him, "Are you the one who paid my bill for therapy?"

"Uh, no. For transparency's sake though, I did try to. But someone beat me to it."

"You really don't have to do that. I have insurance."

"Well, it doesn't matter, does it? I didn't. So there's no fight to be had about it."

"You just aren't gonna bite no matter what I cast, are you?"

"Nope. I am in no mood to fight. Especially with someone in such a state as… this." He pointed at her head then moved his fingers down and back up the length of her body. "No gentleman would do such a thing."

"Aww, You hear that, Lorna. You got yourself a real Prince Charming." Somehow she managed a twinkle in her eye, even through the fog of medication and pain.

"Well, I've had to live with an evil step-sister long enough. I think I've earned it."

A low, rumbling laugh came from Kahrren's chest. "Nice one." She raised her brows in Lorna's direction. "That's how it's done, pretty boy."

"You two truly have a dysfunctional relationship…" Shaking his head and grinning, he picked up his mug of tea. "but somehow you fit together. You're the best example of complimentary opposites I can think of." He saw Kahrren look at him, then smile. The trio had truly become fond of each other. He smiled back.

* * *

Lab results took longer than Adams would have liked, particularly since they provided no actionable information. Most of the fibers were identifiable in source but utterly impossible to associate with a person. There were no traces of blood from the victim, suggesting the resin encasement was done off site, which was something anyone could have assumed. All of the evidence collected led them exactly nowhere.

Sharp heard from Arnie on a daily basis, but to the point this day's phone call was received, the only progress was information about the block being reduced to a shell around the body, allowing for imaging to begin. "He's done multiple CT scans and MRIs. He wants to make sure he won't need anything else in case removing the body screws up any evidence," he told Rodriguez.

"Well, here is the list of people whose prints they pulled up. These can be quick phone calls to see when they were at the museum. Don't bother going out to talk to anyone unless you have a good reason."

"Yep. We'll get on this."

"Hey. I know this sucks. And I know you probably won't get anywhere. I know you're doing the best you can with what you have."

"Thanks, Lieutenant." Sharp showed his appreciation with a firm nod, and returned to his desk, facing the kid. "Prints. Rodriguez said we can call. There's no need to go out to interview unless we find cause. These probably won't get us anywhere. But...every lead, right?"

"That's right." He took the pages offered by Sharp. The calling began.

About ten minutes in, Rodriguez came out and waited for the detectives to disconnect. "We got a body."

"Thank God," the kid said as he stood up, snatching his jacket.

Sharp grabbed his coat and grinned at Rodriguez. "Kids. Can't sit still. Don't know the real meaning of police work." Rodriguez chuckled.

Adams responded with Sharp's classic, "Shaddup."

"Think it's the same guy?" Sharp held up the list of people he'd been calling.

Rodriguez shook his head. "As far as I know this is a stand alone incident. But, what you've got *there* is a lot of busy work, and there's no one else around. Take a break from the calls for a while and go check this out. If we get any evidence about the cube case, I'll put someone else on this one and you two will go back to this."

Sharp nodded and turned to the door with Adams on his heel.

* * *

A shrill cry from the master bedroom penetrated the walls, launching Lorna and Andrew out of bed. Lorna reached Kahrren's room at superhuman speed, placing a hand on her shrieking friend. She gently shook Kahrren who was curled up into a fetal position, holding her head, emitting a steady stream of shrieks and moans. "Kahrren! Wake up!" No jolt came from her body, indicating she was waking from a nightmare. No such luck in this case. Andrew flipped on the hallway light allowing a dim illumination of the faces in the room. Kahrren's eyes were open.

"Kahrren, *what* is wrong?"

"It won't stop. Oh, God, it won't stop." Kahrren squeezed her eyes closed and pressed her hands into the side of her head. Lorna looked over her shoulder at Andrew, panicked.

"Andrew, call 9-1-1. Kahrren, what won't stop?"

"The noise. The talking. The pain." Her sobs were uncontrolled as she reached for the medication on her nightstand. Lorna reached and grabbed the pill bottle, dispensing the maximum dose safe for someone of Kahrren's size. "*No* ambulance. No 9-1-1!"

"You're out of your mind," Lorna said. "There could be something wrong with your brain."

"I called. They're on their way anyway. I'll call her neurologist and tell him we are heading to the hospital." Andrew got dressed as he phoned the doctor. Lorna was dressed already, having developed the habit of sleeping in her clothes in case of an incident like this one.

Five and a half hours later, the exhausted trio returned home with all new prescriptions and directions in hand, having been informed at length about how far off Kahrren's medication levels were.

Having carried Kahrren to bed, well medicated and completely exhausted, Andrew followed Lorna out of her room. "What a shit show. I can't believe the level of incompetence we saw today." Andrew didn't get angry often, but somehow the screaming agony of the woman who was now as good as a sister, and the distress his one true love had to endure during the course of the evening was unacceptable. "I have half a mind to go down there and raise some hell tomorrow. Unbelievable."

"Yes. Something needs to change. Can we talk about it when we wake up?"

"Let me change the voicemail for the office and reschedule a few things I was supposed to do this morning. I'll be to bed in a minute." He kissed Lorna and cleared his morning, then fell into bed next to her, utterly exhausted.

* * *

Wednesday

"No, ma'am. The power was out over almost the whole city. There were no cameras operational at the time this occurred." Adams had given this explanation to dozens of people over the days it took to conduct telephone interviews with museum patrons. He wrapped up the call after a few more questions and unresponsive answers. He set down the receiver and looked at Sharp. "I'm done with the list. How about you?"

"Almost. But we called it. This is getting us nowhere."

Rodriguez walked out of his office and toward the desks at which Adams and Sharp sat, facing each other. He set the paper in front of Sharp, on the desk. "Lab stuff. Nothing we can use. Anything from the phone calls?"

"No, sir. It's been a dead end."

"You guys have any leads or ideas you wanna try? I'm open to pretty much anything at this point." The lieutenant was an open-minded man on any day, but the bizarre nature of this crime had everyone baffled and grasping at straws. The detectives shook their heads. They had chased down every possible lead based on physical evidence. "Okay. I want you to go talk to that massage girl."

"You what?" Neither man could believe what their dignified generally reasonable superior officer had suggested, but Sharp, in particular, was stunned.

"Sir, even if she could tell us anything, would we be able to act on it? How do we explain where we got the information for any lead she provides? Is it a good idea?" Adams had a point.

"You got a better one?"

Adams blew out a breath. "No, sir."

"Then, enjoy your trip through the city. Let me worry about explaining the details."

Grabbing their coats, they headed to the car.

"Is she back at her apartment?" Sharp knew the kid had checked in on Kahrren regularly.

"It's been a while since I called but last I heard she was still at her friend's place."

"Should we call first?"

Adams recited his idea of what such a call would sound like. "Hi Kahrren, can we come beg you to help us with your psychic abilities on this case we picked up with no evidence?"

"All right, kid. No need to get *sharp* on me," he said, at once shutting the kid down and recognizing himself as being an old grump.

"Ha! I see what you did there! Who knew you were funny? Sharp. I like that." The kid flashed his million dollar smile. "Let's try Lorna's, I guess."

"Yep. I'll drive."

A short while later, having stood outside the door to Lorna's townhouse for several minutes with no response, they returned to the car.

"Could she have gone back to work?" Sharp asked.

"I doubt it. Last I heard she was still in pretty bad shape."

"Any idea where she could be?"

"Should we check Andrew Glenn's office? Maybe she hangs out there?"

"Worth a try." Sharp directed the car in the direction of the office. When they arrived, the doors were locked, and the lights were off. "Are we gonna have to file a missing person report on top of everything else?"

"Maybe we should check her apartment?"

"Can't we just call? I don't see the point of driving over the whole city to find her when there is an easier way."

"I suppose you want *me* to call? Since you have the number and aren't dialing…"

"Great detective work, Adams. There's hope for you after all."

"You are less amusing every day, Jim."

"So I am told."

Adams pulled out his cell phone as they walked to where the car was parked on the street. After a few moments he spoke. "Hi Kahrren, it's Mitch Adams. I'm calling to check in on you and see how things are going. Detective Sharp and I would like to come by and see you as soon as you're up for it if that's okay. Gimme a call back. Bye."

"So now what?"

"Start driving. I'll call Lorna." He swiped through the contacts on his phone until he found her number. "Hi Lorna, it's Mitch Adams."

"Oh, hi. What can I do for you?"

"I'm trying to reach Kahrren to make sure she is okay. Is she around?"

"She is at therapy. She goes Monday, Wednesday, and Friday. She won't be done until around one."

"Okay. How's she doing?"

"Honestly, it's been a rough week."

"I hope everything is okay."

"Well, we've got her back to some semblance of normal after a visit to the hospital. Her medication levels were way off, and she was having problems. Also, they worked her really hard at physical therapy on Monday. She was in bad shape. She is still in pretty bad shape from it. I had to go in there this morning and tell the guy to dial it back."

"Jeeze. I'm really sorry to hear that. Is she still staying with you?"

"Yes, she is."

Mitch nodded the affirmation to Sharp. "All right. Would it be okay if we stop by later?"

"I think you'd better ask her. Try calling her after two. She should be home by then."

"Thank you, Lorna. Much appreciated."

"You're welcome. Bye."

Mitch spun his phone in his hand and slipped it into his pocket. "Therapy. She said try calling after two. Know what that means?" Mitch flashed his teeth and chomped them together while wiggling his eyebrows. "Let's eat."

"I swear, kid. You eat more than anyone I've ever met."

"That's because I work out three times as much. It makes me hungry. But I'll let you pick what we're having today."

* * *

That evening, having had a less taxing mid-week physical therapy session as a result of Lorna's insistence on walking her friend into the office for her appointment, Kahrren was in far better shape than her previous appointment had left her. The walker set aside, she had returned to using the cane, and was again starting to maneuver without it. Still, she was slow, and Lorna beat her to the door. "You ready?"

"Yep."

The door opened to reveal Mitch's smiling face, and an almost pleasant look on Sharp's. "Hey, look at you! You're looking a lot better than the last time we saw you." Mitch entered the townhouse in response to Lorna's sweeping arm, followed by Sharp, who managed a polite smile. "Thanks," Mitch said.

"Hello, gentlemen." Kahrren finally arrived at the entry to greet the visitors. "Please come in and have a seat." Lorna kept an eye on her to be sure she made it to the living room, then disappeared to get refreshments. The trio left in the lounge exchanged pleasantries, all involved obviously happy to see one another.

"You look good, kid. I don't know about Mitch, but I haven't seen ya since the hospital."

"No, I haven't seen her either. You look worlds better, Kahrren."

"Thanks. I feel quite a bit better, but as you can see, I still struggle." She kicked at her cane lightly, then winced. "Ow. I'm a bit sore from therapy this week."

"Do the doctors expect you to be able to work again?" Sharp had a way of cutting straight to the point.

"I get the distinct *impression* that they're surprised I lived at all. The answer they give me when I ask about it is along the lines of 'We'll have to wait and see'." She shrugged. In truth, she knew exactly what they were thinking. *You'll never massage again and you're damn lucky you're even breathing, much less walking.*

"So you have a lot of time on your hands, then?" Sharp's face lifted in inquiry.

"Tell me, Jim. Is there a reason you're asking?" With the advantage Kahrren had, she was surprised he was trying this roundabout approach to asking something of her.

The corner of his mouth came up, derisively. "You mean you don't know?"

"Of course she knows, Jim. Look at her face," Adams shifted in his seat in a demonstration of the discomfort he was feeling in asking.

"Of course I know. But it's more polite to have the conversation, isn't it?" Pressing her lips together, she held Sharp's gaze, returning his challenge.

Holding a silver plated tray presenting lemonade, water, and coffee, Lorna returned to the living room and placed it on the coffee table. "Something to drink, gentlemen?"

"Sharp will have coffee, black. Adams will take water even though he wants lemonade." Kahrren ignored their surprised visages. She no longer felt up to pretending. "And I'm sorry. I am not up to helping you with your investigation."

Lorna handed drinks to their guests, then poured coffee for Kahrren and herself. As she set Kahrren's mug before her, she commented, "I can't believe you'd even ask her, seeing the shape she's in. And especially after I told you how rough it's been for her this week."

Unable to suppress her smile, Kahrren put her hand on Lorna's forearm, halting further commentary. "Thank you for the coffee, Lorna. And it's fine. I've got this." She picked up her coffee as Lorna sat with her own. "They didn't want to come. Rodriguez made them."

"And who is Rodriguez?" Lorna asked.

Screwing the cap onto his water bottle, Adams said, "Our boss, Lieutenant Marco Rodriguez." Tapping the half empty bottle on his leg, he sat back, looking embarrassed. "We are at a dead end with this case. No physical evidence. No witnesses. The power was out from the big storm, so there were no cameras to capture any security footage."

"Hell, we don't even have an ID on the victim yet because the medical examiner is still trying to get the body out of the resin." Sharp set his coffee on the coaster Lorna laid out for him. "Is there anything you can tell us?"

"I am really not up for this. It's an awful lot of darkness you're asking me to jump into. And in case you hadn't noticed, I'm not really in any shape for plyometrics of any kind, metaphysical or otherwise." She paused for a moment to collect her thoughts. "Besides I think my dad wouldn't have wanted me to get involved. And I think I finally understand why."

"I think your Dad would understand, Kahrren." Sharp appeared to let the comment escape his mouth before he considered the implication. He stared at Kahrren's face, seemingly to avoid looking at Mitch.

Kahrren did not miss Mitch's look of surprise. Or how his head became a vortex of scrutiny of what his partner said, or evidently failed to say. Her tone became firmer. "I need you to honor my choice. I don't want to be a part of this. I am struggling to make it from day to day as it is."

Mitch took a long pull off his water bottle then set it on the coaster laid for him. "Okay, what about if you don't actively help, but we just come to you? Maybe we could bring something over for you to hold and pick up some information?"

Lorna stood abruptly and marched to the door. "That's enough. It's time for you to leave. She has given you her answer. Three times! Now I'd like you to leave my house."

"We're very sorry to have bothered you." Rising to exit, Adams looked back at Kahrren. "I wish you the very best in your recovery." Nodding in agreement, Sharp uttered a polite goodbye to each of the women, and the two detectives departed.

As Adams opened the car door, he froze. "Hey, Jim?"

"Yeah?"

"Did you notice something funny about the drink...assignments Karren gave us?"

"Yeah."

"Like she didn't have to touch anything to, uh... what does she call it?"

"Sense."

"Yes." He frowned at Sharp. "But you're not surprised. Which kind of makes me think you knew already."

"Come on kid. Let's go." Sharp settled in the car and fastened his seatbelt, waiting for Adams. Mitch installed himself into the passenger seat, appearing unsettled. "So why didn't you tell me you knew her dad?"

"Ah, shit, kid. We gotta do this now?"

"You'd prefer I sit with it and stew for a long while, allowing my anger to fester because you've been keeping something from me?"

"Yes, I would. I don't want to talk about this."

"You're a real dick."

Acknowledging the statement, Sharp nodded, aloof, then merged the car into the stream of traffic flowing past.

* * *

After seeing the detectives to the door, Lorna headed to her bedroom, leaving Kahrren alone in the living room. She sat back and closed her eyes.

"Wow. That was kind of rude." Brittany had become disturbingly more judgmental in death. "I'd think you'd be willing to help the men who *literally* saved your life."

Kahrren carefully maneuvered herself back onto the cushions. "Hey, Brittany?"

"Yeah?"

"Drop dead." The laugh which emanated from the already dead woman pierced Kahrren, through and through. "Ugh. Don't laugh like that. It's… It feels…" She was losing steam quickly.

"Penetrating?"

"Ew, dirty." She wrinkled her nose on one side. "I was gonna go with yucky, but you're not wrong." She clutched a pillow and closed her eyes. "I need some rest. Go solve the murder or something, will ya?" She waited for a response from the apparition. When none came, she cracked an eye open to find herself alone. She uttered a brief word of relief and fell asleep.

Chapter Four

Friday

It was a good idea to schedule her massage after her physical therapy. The massage helped alleviate the effects of the hard work she had put in, despite Lorna's objection. On her way out, she even managed to keep a calm head when stopping to inquire about her bill. "Hi, Julie. I need to know who paid my bill."

"Oh. Well, they asked me not to tell you that."

"I am sure they did. However, it is my right to know." She looked at the receptionist expectantly. The phone rang and Julie flashed her an unapologetic look and said, "Sorry, but I have to get this," and picked up the receiver. With her attention focused on the caller, Julie's defenses came down, and Kahrren got exactly what she was after, if not the answer she was expecting, by probing her mind. There *was* no bill. None of the practitioners at Thrive billed for any of their services. She was simultaneously touched and angry. Each one of them was going to lose a fortune in helping her out. *That's what friends are for, I guess.*

"I'll see you on Monday!" Julie was cheerful, and clearly, also relieved when Kahrren turned to walk out.

Kahrren made it out to the parking lot on her own. A few moments later, a bright yellow blur of flower power halted in front of her. "Hey, hot stuff!

You looking for a good time?"

In the flattest voice she could present, she looked at her friend and said, "I *am* the good time, honey." Kahrren stepped carefully into Lorna's new Volkswagen Beetle, clicked her seatbelt in place, and allowed herself to grin at their exchange. "You are hopelessly cheerful."

"Why, thank you."

"That was not a compliment."

"I know and don't even care a little." She zipped off into the streets of Portland. "You want me to drop you home or you want to come to the office for a bit?"

"I can come to the office, but can we make a stop first?"

"Yeah. Where to?"

"Portland Police Department."

Lorna's face was a dance of expressions. Her face contorted like it was in Cirque du Soleil, showing surprise, chagrin, understanding, and misgiving. "Are you sure?"

"Yes. I am sure." She let out a short, soft chuckle. "Brittany, of all people, or unpeople… brought up a good point."

"Stop. Wait. Your statement does not track. Brittany doesn't make good points. Also, why are you taking advice from dead people?"

"Because, in some weird cosmic twist, Brittany has become smarter in death. And as much as it pains me, she called me out. Hard."

"How did she accomplish such a feat?"

After a demonstrative sigh of exasperation, Kahrren revealed, "She essentially told me I was an ingrate for not helping the men who literally saved my life."

"I mean, she has a point."

"I know, right?" Kahrren made her voice bubbly and high-pitched to imitate the trendy use of the phrase which had lately surfaced in the post-millennial zeitgeist. Grinning at Lorna who was giggling at the mockery, she continued, "She may be a wretched pain in my ass, but she does have a point."

"Hiiiiiiiiiieeeeeeeeee, Kaaaahrreeen! I heard that!" The appearance of the specter in question startled Kahrren into a pronounced, if brief, convulsion of surprise, which in turn startled the tiny blonde driver beside her.

"Jeeze! What the *hell*, Kahrren?" Looking at her passenger Lorna observed Kahrren's right hand on the glass of the window, her left on the center divider, and practically her entire body pushed into the small space between the seat and the side panel of the car. She was far more startled than Lorna.

Moving her right hand from the pane of glass to lay flatly over her heart, she screeched, "Brittany you scared the shit out of me!"

"Tell her if she wasn't already dead, I'd kill her right now!" Lorna's face was reddening as she shook her head and her voice was intermittently interrupted with laughter.

"Tell her I can hear her." Brittany purposely laughed her most annoying laugh. "So where are we going, Kahrren? Hmmmmmmmmm?"

"She says she can hear you. And she is taunting me about where we are going," she said to Lorna. She turned her head toward the back seat and growled, "I am going to the police station to help them with their stupid case, and *you* are going away."

"Oooh, *really*? Who gave you the brilliant idea of helping the cops, hmm?" She purposely dragged out the questions in a sing-song voice.

Kahrren straightened her body in her seat, returning to a forward facing position. "You did. And if you still think I should go, you ought to leave me to it before I change my mind out of sheer spite for your botheration."

Together, Lorna and Brittany asked, "Is that even a word?"

"Yes, it's a word." Kahrren swished her hand through the air where Brittany's torso was, eliciting a spectral shriek.

With a cry of "Rude!" Brittany disappeared.

Kahrren looked at Lorna. "She doesn't like it when someone moves through her." She shot a wicked grin at Lorna who looked completely befuddled at having witnessed only one side of the exchange. "So I make it a point to do it as frequently as I can."

* * *

On an average day a police station was a bustling environment. On this day though, the people inside were positively reeling. Holding her cane in her left hand, she placed her right hand around Lorna's arm as they looked around. "The energy in here is awful. What's going on?" Lorna barely had time to get her question out when a massive, intimidating, uniform-clad man walked in with several similarly uniformed men following him. "Oh."

From behind a moustache, an authoritative and articulate basso profundo asked, "Have you ladies been assisted?" The gargantuan man stood six and a half feet tall, dwarfing everyone around him. Kahrren turned to the man, dropped her cane, and threw herself into his arms. *"Well..."* The Chief of Police chuckled at her display of affection. "I didn't expect to see you here, Miss." His booming voice lowered to a whisper. "Kahrren, I'm here in an official capacity. Would you mind if we take this somewhere more private in a few minutes?"

"Shut up, Bub." Though she was grinning, tears streamed down her face. She hadn't seen her godfather since her stay in the hospital. The officers surrounding the chief were stirring as if preparing to assist in her removal. He waved them off with one arm and held her firmly with the other.

"Yes, Miss." From behind his grin his concern and affection were obvious. "Did you get my flowers?"

"Mmmhmm." Kahrren detached herself from the hulking man. "Also, the candy, the singing telegram, the cards, the voice mails. All of it. Thank you." She gazed up at him with nothing but adoration in her eyes.

"You are welcome. Now, tell me why you're here." He looked down at her expectantly. "And who is your bodyguard?" He winked at Lorna who was standing as tall as possible. The man absolutely dwarfed her.

"It's a long story, Bub. But today I want to see the detectives who saved me."

Lorna proffered Kahrren the cane she retrieved from the floor after its unplanned flinging across the lobby, which Kahrren took. "I'm Lorna Landry, sir. I'm Kahrren's best friend and roommate." She confidently held her hand out to shake. Delicately taking her tiny paw in his enormous clutch, they shook. "And may I have the pleasure of your name?" The woman was unflinching, but she had the advantage of years of stories about Bub and knew him to be a gentle giant.

"Miss Landry, I'm so very pleased to meet you. My name is Robert Donovan, and I run this little circus." He nodded beyond the women to the stable of suspended law enforcement officers staring at the exchange from behind them. "I'm the Chief of Police."

"Well, I'm very pleased to finally make your acquaintance. Please call me Lorna."

"Yes, Miss Lorna. I am pleased to finally meet you, as well. I have heard so very much about you from Little Miss Sunshine here." He and Lorna both looked at Kahrren with playful condescension. "I call her Miss, for short." They had come to the same nickname independently, and Kahrren knew she would get no end of shit for the coincidence.

"I call her Little Miss Sunshine, too. Because... well, look at her." Kahrren scowled at Lorna and turned her head in dismissal. Her all black wardrobe and hair, paired with the gesture, proved Lorna's point nicely.

Bub chuckled. "Well, Miss Lorna, it seems we have a lot to talk about. Would you two join me for dinner sometime?"

"We'd love to. Thank you. Shall I call to schedule with your assistant?"

"That will do nicely. I'll let her know to expect your call." He looked at Kahrren. "You'll let me know when you're finished with your meeting?" It was more of a command than a request. She answered with a nod and stepped back to let him resume his duties. The stable of men surrounding him all sharpened and followed when he started to move through the station. Every law enforcement affiliated personage in the room followed suit.

"So I guess we know why everyone was in a panic when we walked in." Lorna playfully bumped Kahrren with her elbow. "Now let's go find Sipowicz and Silver Spoons."

The scrambling which ensued in the wake of the chief walking through the offices was of epic proportion. Lorna appeared amused watching the people skitter from one task to the next. Kahrren, however, was having an increasingly difficult time, demonstrated by her slowed pace and increased squinting. She grabbed onto Lorna's arm to steady herself. "You all right?"

Lorna wrapped an arm around Kahrren's shoulders.

"I gotta get out of this room. Take me over there." She pointed to an empty office on the periphery of the giant, open space. "Then can you go get them?"

Almost humming her agreement, she walked Kahrren to a chair as they entered. Together they helped her ease down into the chair, eliciting a groan from each of them.

"Ooof. You're having salad for dinner."

"You're not even a little funny. I'll eat your sofa first." Kahrren had never been a big fan of vegetables. Eating nothing but green stuff for a meal was out of the question. Lorna giggled as she walked out of the room to find her targets.

She wandered through the area looking through the sea of faces in the chaotic scene. It took a couple of moments but she spotted Sharp's funky, old leather jacket hanging over a chair. Heading toward it, she was suddenly stopped when Adams stepped in front of her.

"Looking for something?" he asked.

She sighed when she recognized him, the creases in her face smoothing.

"It's kind of a…" He looked around the room, *"really* bad time."

"I'm looking for you and your partner. Kahrren is here and has decided to talk to you. She is in pretty bad shape, or I would bring her back later."

"How bad?"

"She grabbed on to me and asked me to help her to a private room."

"Dammit. Why couldn't she have called like a normal person?"

"That's a good question, actually. I should've thought of that." Lorna's head tilted as a smile grew on her face. She shrugged. "But since we're here, can you grab Sharp and give her a few minutes?"

He nervously ran his tongue over his teeth under closed lips. "Yeah. I'll go find him. But I can't guarantee how much time we'll get."

"Oh, well, I think if you consider the fact that the big, scary Police Chief is her godfather, you can find a way to come up with as much time as she asks for."

He shook his head in dismay. "You have got to be kidding me." He shifted his weight onto one leg and placed his hand on the same side hip. "I guess since her dad worked here, it makes sense she would know him, but I had no idea he was her godfather."

"Yup. And she isn't afraid of him one bit. She told him to shut up in front of the whole department. The way I hear it, he is wrapped around her little finger."

"Oh, good. How reassuring." Exasperated, he turned and recruited Sharp.

As he approached, following Adams, Lorna greeted him, not bothering to camouflage the less than friendly feelings she had toward him. "Detective."

"Ms. Landry." Sharp nodded to her without any appearance of hard feelings or dislike. During the ordeal concerning Derek Martin, the man who killed Brittany and almost killed Kahrren, Lorna was steadfast in supporting the people she cared about, resulting in several encounters where she told him off and didn't hold back. She liked to think that he respected her for it.

Lorna led them into the room where Kahrren waited to find her leaning forward with her head on the table. She placed her hand on Kahrren's back. "You okay?"

"Christ, you look awful," Sharp spewed when he saw her. He took a step toward her, then paused. He turned and left the room in haste and returned with a bottle of water. "Drink."

She took the bottle and tried to twist the cap. She couldn't. Adams gently took the bottle from her, opened it, and handed it back. "Here ya go. Are you sure you want to talk today? We can come to you another day. It really looks like you should rest."

Kahrren sipped and nodded her head. Then shook it, rotating left and right. "I thought I could. Now I'm not so sure."

"*What do you mean psychic?*" The booming yell permeated through all of the walls in the place. Chief Donovan's voice could not be contained by the mere mortal construct of walls. "*What kind of horseshit are you trying to feed me, Rodriguez?*"

"Uh oh." Adams peeked through the privacy blinds covering the window. "Sounds like Big Boss isn't buying what the lieutenant is selling."

The blustering continued, "*Are you trying to tell me you haven't been able to find one damn clue in the most heinous, demented case I have seen in my entire career?"*

"Shit," Kahrren said. "The cat's about to come out of the bag."

"What do you mean?" Lorna tried to stop Kahrren from rising.

"No. I have to do this." She pulled herself up, gripped her cane and started heading toward the source of the shouting.

Adams and Sharp both followed Kahrren in what would have been considered a chase, had she been able to move fast enough. Their attempts to deter her failed miserably. "Kahrren, he has a notorious temper. You should not go in there." Sharp had maneuvered himself in front of her and threw his hands up in front of her forcefully.

"If you don't move, I will accidentally beat you to death with my cane." She paused for a moment and leaned on the cane, grateful for a moment to rest before continuing her migration.

"Fine. You can face the consequences. I hope you like jail." Sharp scoffed, then saw Adams grin knowingly. "What's so funny, kid?"

"Oh, we share secrets now? I had no idea. I am perfectly willing to share mine if you come out with yours."

"Quid pro quo? Really?"

Adams shrugged. "Your rules. I'm just playing the game." He turned away from Sharp, who turned the other direction.

Finding an opportunity in the distraction, Kahrren proceeded with Lorna at her side. Reaching the door, she knocked three times, hard. She was duly ignored, but it was no matter, as she turned the handle anyway.

"Who the *hell* are you? And what are you doing in my office?"

Kahrren met Rodriguez's attack with only a look of warning, which was entirely ignored, and unnecessary in any case, as the chief interjected in an ominous tone. His speech slowed down to a menacing crawl as he puffed up to his full height and breadth. "That is my goddaughter, and the child of Alex McClintock, and you will not speak to her that way again."

The color drained from Rodriguez's face. "I am very sorry, Ms. McClintock. I'm sorry, Chief. I didn't know." Rodriguez wiped his hand across his forehead and took a calming breath. "How may I help you?" He paused, displaying a look of confusion as something dawned on him. Kahrren's eyes bulged and she shook her head frantically trying to stop what he was about to say. "Wait, sir. You know the psychic?"

"The what?"

Chapter Five

S till Friday

Rodriguez looked at Sharp. Sharp looked at Adams. Adams looked at Lorna. In turn, they exchanged glances indicating bafflement, worry, amusement, and even alarm as the volume of the conversation raised and softened behind the door of Rodriguez's office. The opposing timbres coming from behind the door alternated between deep rumbling and ear-piercingly shrill.

"Let me know when they're done in there. I'm going to go calm my nerves with some coffee." Rodriguez walked toward the break room, evidently feeling a bit put out for having been excused from his own office.

"What the hell is going on?" Sharp looked at Lorna, inquiring of her. "The kid won't tell me."

"The chief's her godfather."

"Well, how about that?" Sharp smirked and seemed happy.

Adams jumped on the comment with a derisive remark of his own. "Oh, you mean you didn't know?"

"What the hell is going on between you two?" Lorna demanded.

"Oh, sorry, Lorna. Sharp has some stuff he is hiding from me and won't tell me what it is. So not only is he destroying my trust in him, he is making working with him a real bummer."

"Well, that's pretty rotten," Lorna agreed. "Why would you do such a thing?"

she inquired of Sharp. Lorna and Adams gave Sharp their full attention, expectantly.

He eyed Adams. "Later, kid. I'll tell you everything later. Looks like we have movement." He nodded toward the office where Donovan's hulking mass and Kahrren's more diminutive stature slowly moved toward one another. Moments later the door opened at the hand of the chief, and revealed his expression of controlled anger, followed by a white-faced, red-eyed, recovering massage therapist.

Kahrren cleared her throat and looked at Lorna. "We'll be hosting the chief for dinner tonight, if you don't mind." She had the look of a reprimanded puppy. "It seems I have some more explaining to do." She looked at Donovan who nodded.

"Will you please take her home? She feels unwell." He directed his comment to Lorna. "And I'll see you around seven, if you're agreeable. I'll take care of dinner."

"Yes, sir. We'll take care of dessert. We look forward to seeing you later." Lorna stepped up to Kahrren, moving to put her arm around her, but Adams beat her to it.

"If you'll excuse me, sir, I'll assist Ms. McClintock to the car." Without waiting, he supported nearly all of Kahrren's weight, virtually carrying her through the station with Lorna trailing.

Donovan's authoritative voice directed Sharp. "Get Rodriguez and both of you get in here. Romeo can join us after he assists my goddaughter to the car." Sharp was a brave man, but not brave enough to utter a single syllable in response. He swiftly moved to carry out the order.

* * *

Donovan greeted Lorna brightly as she opened the door to his full arms. Andrew stepped from behind her to take some of the load as Lorna introduced him. "Robert Donovan, this is my boyfriend, Andrew Glenn. Andrew, this is Kahrren's godfather and the Chief of Police, Robert Donovan."

"Robert is perfectly fine." He nodded an acknowledgment to Andrew and thanked him for lightening his load.

"Very nice to meet you, sir. Please let me take these for you. Kahrren is in the living room, resting on the couch." With a smile of gratitude, Robert handed over the remaining bags to Lorna and Andrew who disappeared with them into the kitchen. As they worked on setting out the food, Bub knelt next to Kahrren.

"Hello, Miss. Are you feeling any better?" He placed his colossal mitt over her forehead and caressed her cheek. "You scared me today. I have never seen you in such an emotional state. Even when you were in the hospital, you were more poised than you were today.

"I know. I'm doing better." The corner of her mouth lifted; the only expression of emotion she could muster. "I didn't mean to worry you. I'm sorry."

"Kahrren, you *cried*. I haven't seen you cry since you were in diapers." He huffed out a breath, exasperated. "And I can't believe some of the things you said to me today."

She sat up, propelled by the resurfacing emotions of their earlier conversation. "Bub, I am so sorry. I was out of line."

He held his hand up, indicating she should say no more. She obeyed his unspoken command and understood the reason for it. He didn't want to fight until after dinner. With his assistance, she made it to the kitchen and to her place at the table, which had been beautifully laid by Andrew and Lorna. At Lorna's invitation, Bub sat to Kahrren's right, facing the door to the kitchen. She learned of this preference from Kahrren, who had, of course, given her unsolicited opinion on how things should go through the course of the evening.

"Ladies and gentleman, everything looks beautiful. There's one problem though." Lorna looked at Kahrren, puzzled, and Kahrren grinned. Picking up the cloth napkins laid out in front of each of the place settings, he said, "These won't do." He rose and set them on the counter, then pulled from his coat a baggie of damp towelettes.

From beneath a depressed eyebrow, Lorna leaned over and removed one of the cardboard lids to the large tin food pans before them. "Well, I wasn't expecting barbecue!" She smiled and licked her lips in anticipation of the best barbecue the city had to offer. The lids came off to reveal ribs, chicken, brisket, baked beans, macaroni and cheese, and coleslaw. There was enough to feed twenty hungry men. Or Kahrren and Lorna.

Andrew chuckled. "Robert, I'd like to invite you to come for dinner as frequently as possible." The group shared a chuckle, and commenced in filling their plates, and bellies, beyond reasonable capacity.

Conversation stayed pleasant throughout the course of dinner, however, when the plates were cleared, the gloves came off. "Now, young lady," Robert started, "You need to start from the beginning and explain this to me. I will do my best to believe you, but I definitely need some clarification."

"Shall we excuse you to have this conversation privately?" Andrew asked Robert. His words offered privacy, however, his tone and raised brows over rounded eyes showed hope that the answer would be no. "That won't be necessary. She told me you two already know about this supposed ability."

"There is nothing supposed about it, Bub. I have had it all my life. My dad told me to keep it a secret from everyone except him." She sat up straighter, demonstrating her confidence in the statement. "My dad believed it was the safest and smartest thing to do and now knowing what I do about how people respond to it, I believe he was right." Kahrren went on to describe what it was like to have her ability while she was growing up, things she knew about Bub he'd never told anyone, and how she had helped her dad find the boy in the barn.

"I knew it!" Bub slapped the table in victory. "I knew he had help but he would never come clean about it." He shook his head at her as his mouth fell open, full of wonderment. "Miss, I always knew you were special, but this is so far beyond what I ever imagined."

"Yeah, lucky me." Her tone was drab as she considered what a royal ass-pain this ability was. She looked at the faces around the table as thoughts of *If I had her ability, I'd...* came flying from every direction. "But, Bub, it's not all it's cracked up to be. It completely sucks to know what people really think of you. Especially when they are nice to your face but think you are a freak show or a weirdo. It's no picnic to be bombarded by the *actual* truth all day long."

"Will you indulge me?" he asked.

Kahrren closed her eyes and pressed her lips together, trying to hide her hurt. *He doesn't believe me,* she realized. She nodded, then lifted her eyes to meet his. "Lorna, can you get him some paper and a pen? He wants to play stump the psychic." His mouth dropped when she used the exact phrase he was thinking. "And he is ready for dessert. He hopes it's cheesecake and he'd like some good coffee to go with it." Lorna eagerly popped out of her seat to take care of dessert. She started the coffee brewing and although she had planned on serving tiramisu, she had cheesecake in the refrigerator, so opted to serve it instead. Andrew helped her, getting plates and silverware ready for serving. After a moment of preparations Lorna set a pen and notepad in front of Robert, then returned to her preparations.

"Now wait just a damn minute!" Bub didn't really know why he was protesting. He only recognized how wrong this all seemed. Like a set up.

"Am I wrong?" She stared at him, challenging.

"No. You're not wrong."

"Guys, when you're done, you get to play too. Why not? What's it to me? I hear it all anyway." She stood from the table and wobbled her way toward the bathroom, without excusing herself. She didn't quite care whether she was being rude. She spent a few moments after her relief and ablutions to allow Robert to finish explaining what he wanted.

When she returned she sat in her chair and started on her cheesecake without a word or a glance at any of them. They sat silently and waited for her to say something. Feeling a little salty, she let them wait. Having finished her portion of dessert, she got up and performed a series of tasks while her three companions stared at her expectantly. First, she connected her phone to the Bluetooth speaker to play a song. Next, she retrieved the coffee pot and refilled Bub's mug out of courtesy, then refilled Lorna's while giving her an annoyed look. She took a spoon from the silverware drawer and returned to her seat. She looked at them from behind a sour face as she hissed a warm breath onto the utensil and did her best to hang it on her nose, slowly removing her hands to allow it to hang for at least a moment, before falling to the table.

"First up from Lorna, we have 'refill my coffee.'" Kahrren nodded toward Lorna indicating she should reveal the note hidden under her plate. "Written in blue ink which I am supposed to also say." She turned to Robert. "Next up we have Bub, with his ridiculous 'perform a parlor trick,' written in silver Sharpie." She looked at him expectantly and waited for him to pull the folded paper revealing his silver scrawled note preceded by the number two.

"Number three from Andrew. 'Play a relevant song on the stereo,' which was written in purple crayon." Picking up her phone, she continued. "That's my favorite part of this little charade, by the way. Here is your song. I'm going to bed. Good night." She kissed the top of Bub's head and walked out as she played Queen and David Bowie's "Under Pressure." Andrew revealed his paper, which was, indeed, written in purple crayon.

Robert looked up at Lorna and Andrew, stunned. "It's all real?" They nodded. Robert sat quietly listening to the song. "Sounds like she is feeling some strain about people expecting things from her and feeling a little helpless. How do we fix it?"

"I'm not sure we can. We have to listen to her and trust she will tell us what she needs." Lorna was used to doing this already, but her male counterparts did not seem so keen on the idea.

Robert was seen to the door after a few more minutes of polite conversation and a staunch refusal of his offer to help clean up. After his departure, Lorna and Andrew tidied the kitchen and went to bed.

* * *

Saturday

The bustle of house cleaning didn't rouse Kahrren, but the ringing of her phone did. Normally she would have turned her ringer off, but she had forgotten the previous night. "Hello?" Her sleepy voice sounded extra crunchy as she answered.

"Hi, Kahrren. It's Mitch. Are you okay?"

"Mmhmm. I was asleep but it's okay. What can I do for you?" The blankets moving around her made a muffling sound as they swished around her and hit the phone. "What time is it, anyway?"

A soft snicker escaped Mitch's lips. "It's two o'clock."

"In the morning?" Her heavy duty blackout curtains prevented any light from getting into the room.

"Uh, no. Two in the afternoon. Would it be better to call you back later?"

"Holy crap. Uh, no. Well… can you hang on a minute… or well, it takes me a minute to get around. Is it okay if I call you back in a few minutes? I have to do my morning… routine."

"Sure. Of course. Speak to you soon."

"Thanks. Talk to you soon." She disconnected and made her way to the restroom. Once finished, she dressed herself and sat at the edge of the bed. She picked up the phone and selected Mitch's name from her recent call log. "Hi. Sorry about the delay. What's up?"

"Hi. First I wanted to check on you to see how you're doing. You gave us all a scare yesterday. In more ways than one."

"Yeah. Yesterday sucked. I think it's why I slept so long. I'm okay though. Well, I'm better today than yesterday, at any rate."

"Good. Jim and I were wondering if we could come to you this weekend? Also, we are both very grateful for your willingness to help. Thank you."

"You're welcome. And yes, you may come this weekend, only let me check with Lorna to see when is a good time. Since it's her house and all."

"Sure. Of course. Do you want to text me when you get it worked out?"

"Yes, I'll do that." They exchanged pleasantries before ending the call, then Kahrren emerged from her bedroom.

"It lives!" Lorna was a bit of a mess from housework but was still cute. It was helpful that she was too, because otherwise she would be harder to deal with. Like puppies who shit on the floor or chew up your stuff. They are tolerable when they misbehave because of their adorableness.

"Morning."

"It isn't." Her grin beamed from behind her grubby facade. "But thanks for playing." Kahrren responded with a twisted face which could be described as unpleasant, as she crept down the hallway into the living room and plopped on the sofa. "Are you hungry?""

"Have we met? Of course I am. I can't believe you let me sleep through two meals. What kind of caretaker are you?" Lorna made a face at Kahrren and disappeared into the kitchen for a few moments, returning with two plates of various leftovers found in the refrigerator. "Here. Stir it to mix in the hot and cold spots."

Kahrren accepted the plate while making a one-sided nose crinkle. "You make it sound so appetizing." She started stirring the individual piles of stuff. Enchilada, baked beans, macaroni and cheese, and something which once resembled a vegetable but was unidentifiable in its current form. "Thanks. I know what almost all of these things are!" she joked. "Really, though. Thank you. I still feel wiped out."

"You're welcome. Andrew went to get coffee so we'll be set in a little while. Do you have any plans for the day? Oh, did I hear your phone ring? Who even makes phone calls anymore?"

"Mmm, coffee. I need it today. And yes, it was my phone. It was Mitch. He wanted to see if it would be okay for them to come by this weekend to finish what we tried to start yesterday. Would it be okay with you?"

"Kahrenn, you live here. You don't have to ask my permission to have people over. But I do appreciate the heads up. I don't like looking grubby when people come over. How long do you think they'll be here? And when are they coming?"

"I said I would let him know. Do you have anything going on this weekend?"

"Not really." She exhibited a pleasant smile but evidently noticed Kahrren's laser focus on her face. "What are you doing? Are you reading my mind?"

"Yep. You guys should go. I am totally fine." She pushed the food around her plate with her fork trying to decide which bite was next. "My medication is good. I am ambulatory. Going to dinner and a movie is a good idea for you guys. I'll even schedule the detectives to come over while you are gone so I am not alone the whole time."

"I don't know, Kahrren, are you sure? What if something happens?

"First of all, nothing will happen. Next, I will have police officers here. They have already demonstrated an aptitude and inclination for saving my life, so I believe they can be trusted. And finally, we have these." She held up her cell phone. "These fancy new devices make it possible to reach people who aren't even in the room with you at a moment's notice."

"You are such an asshole."

"Thank you very much." The smile reached all the way to Kahrren's eyes. "Seriously, though. Go to the movies. You can turn your ringer off but leave your phone out so you will see the phone if it rings or if you get a text. It's a win-win."

"Okay. But only because Sharp and Adams will be here. And you have to ask them to stay the whole time." Lorna held up her index finger indicating her seriousness.

"Okay, no. That's silly. I am fine. I will let you know when they get here and when they leave, but I am not asking them to stay longer than they need to." She took another bite, and continued, "Lorna, please do this. Even if it's a couple of hours. We have to start working toward this. I have made sure to ask you when I need help and now I am asking you to give a little and leave the house for an evening. It needs to happen."

"Okay. I will do it on one more condition."

"Which is what?"

"You stop talking with food in your mouth."

Kahrren pressed her lips together pointedly while she finished chewing and swallowed. From her freshly vacated gob, she uttered, "Deal."

* * *

It took a couple of minutes for Kahrren to get to the door when her guests arrived in the evening. Lorna and Andrew left a short while before the detectives arrived making the lag time between someone getting from the couch to the door about triple. The door slowly opened as she tried to get out of its way. "Hi. Come in."

Sharp grumbled, "You didn't ask who was at the door? You just opened it? Seems like you'd be more careful."

"Ah, gee, Dad. I'll be more careful next time. You sure do have a good point. Except, not really because first of all, I'm *psychic,* so I knew you were there, *and* second, you made arrangements to come, so I was expecting you."

Sharp looked at Adams with impatience showing on his face. "I like her better unconscious." He winked at Kahrren, affirming her interpretation that he was kidding.

"That's how we prefer you too, Jim." Adams gave a wry smile which was copied by Kahrren and Sharp alike. "Thanks for agreeing to see us, Kahrren. I know it's been a rough week."

"Sure. Come on in. There's water on the table. Help yourselves to anything else you'd like. Please excuse the self-serve option. It's hard to carry much."

"No problem. Water is fine, thanks." Mitch commented as he led the way to the living room. Kahrren followed slowly behind, settled into her spot against the arm of the couch, and the gentlemen took their seats, facing her. "Are you sure you're feeling up to this today?"

"Yep. I feel pretty good after sleeping most of the day. Besides, I made Lorna leave for the evening, so this is the best time to do it, really."

"Ah, good. I know she has been staying close since the incident happened."

"Very close. She is in desperate need of a break, so I made her go. She had conditions, though." She lifted her phone and tilted it back and forth, indicating she had to send a message. She quickly tapped it out then focused back on the conversation. "So, what do you have for me?"

Sharp held up the file with all the details of the case. "Will you actually need this?"

She shrugged. "It couldn't hurt." Holding out her hand, she waited for Sharp to come to her. He rose and placed the file in her grasp, then returned to his seat. She opened it and started going through the documents. "Yikes. It's kind of gruesome, isn't it?" She continued her perusal of the papers then looked up. "Do you have anything from the crime scene I could touch?"

"I thought you didn't have to touch things anymore," Sharp queried.

"Yeah, that seems to be true when I am around someone, but I guess proximity is an issue. Sorry. I haven't experimented with the way it works since it changed.

"It's all right. Kid, you got the evidence bag?"

"Yep." Adams pulled it out of his coat and stood to hand it to her. "Here ya go."

"Thanks." She held the bag in her hands and closed her eyes. She inhaled deeply, focusing on the item in the bag, a chunk of resin from the block the body was found in. The corner of her mouth pulled down in disappointment. "Huh. Weird. All I am getting is stuff about Mitch." She opened her eyes, passing the bagged resin back and forth between hands. "Maybe because you were holding it." She set it down on the coffee table and picked up a glass of water from beside it.

"Has anything like this ever happened before? Getting the wrong information?" Sharp asked.

Kahrren elevated her shoulder in a one-sided shrug. "Well, it's like I told you before. I can't control what I get when I touch something. Sometimes it's helpful information. Sometimes it is completely random. It seems like in this instance, it's random stuff I'm picking up from *him*," she inclined her head toward the younger cop. "I'll try again. There must be something we can get."

"When did you tell us?" Sharp seemed to have high expectations since learning about her ability. Now, he was a believer, it seemed.

"When we were at Andrew's office during the Sarah Donis murder investigation."

"I see. Okay. Well, is there anything we can do to help you?"

"You wanna go under the kitchen sink and get the Psychic Polish? We can shine it up and see if it works any better." She stared at him deadpan for a moment before her face cracked into a snide smile. "No. There's nothing we can do. If I wasn't getting anything at all, I'd say taking it out of the plastic might help, but I am getting lots of images and info. The problem is it's about something else."

Mitch's countenance darkened at the mention of the visions being related to him. "What are you picking up about me?"

Kahrren's eyes lowered to the floor. She waited a moment, then met his gaze and said, "It's mostly stuff related to when you were a boy. You know when you met my dad?" Her face was soft and concerned, showing none of the caustic temperament for which she was known. "Do you want to hear about it?"

"Definitely not. Let's leave that out of the picture."

"No problem." Having finished her water, she set the glass back down on the table and picked up the resin chunk. A few moments passed in silence behind closed eyes. She started moving her face around, then lifted her lids to look at them. "I'm very sorry. I keep picking up on the same stuff. Umm, Mitch, how much of what we talked about is... *known* to him?""

Mitch's only answer was rotating his head slowly from left to right. "I haven't told him much. I don't plan to."

Sharp huffed in exasperation. "You don't have to, kid. I know what happened." The look on his face was conflicted, as if he simultaneously felt a heavy weight had been lifted from his chest, but landed on his brows and jowls, pulling them downward in guilt. "I was there."

"Come again?" Mitch sat forward, elbows on thighs. "What the hell do you mean you were there?"

"The barn, kid. I was there when you were rescued from the barn. Alex McClintock was my partner. I was there. I know everything."

Mitch shot out of his chair and stood in a wide stance, arms slightly spread apart in a fighting pose. Then he froze. His face reddened first from embarrassment, then from rage. He was panting his wrath, waiting for Sharp to explain how he had misunderstood. The explanation never came. "That's not true. It can't be. You would have told me. *Someone* would have told me!" He raked his fingers through his hair and started to move around the living room. Despite his regimented lifestyle and years of therapy consistently serving to keep his shit together, he was overcome by this revelation. He started to weep. "No. *God, no!* Tell me it's not true." He stood over the older man, who remained seated. "Jim, please… tell me it's not true." He stepped back and placed his fist over his mouth, failing to control his sob.

Sharp stood and walked over to him. He reached out, trying to place a hand on his shoulder to calm or comfort the younger cop, he wasn't sure which. The gesture was met with a flinch and brisk step backward by Adams. "Come on, Mitch. It's not a big deal. I didn't want to embarrass you, is all."

"How could you? Keeping this from me was so far beyond wrong, I can't even begin to describe it. What else haven't you told me?" Agony spilled down his face in the form of tears. His arms crossed over his torso in a protective posture.

Sharp shook his head back and forth. "Mitch, come on. You gotta calm down. This isn't why we're here." He evidently took the physical cues from Adams and stepped backward as he spoke in a soothing voice to his partner.

"What else, Jim?" His voice was loud, high-pitched, and sounded a bit caught in his throat. "I can see in your face there's more."

"I've been keeping an eye on ya, that's all."

"What *exactly* do you mean?" His tone was becoming increasingly desperate.

Sharp sighed and plopped back into his chair, his hand raising up to cover his eyes for a moment, then wiped at his face in a seemingly familiar nervous gesticulation. Hesitating, he revealed, "I always kept an eye on you from the time you were a kid. I watched out for ya all the way through school, even college. When you applied to the police academy, I put in a good word. Stuff I didn't think would be a big deal."

"Are you the reason I got promoted so fast?" Mitch's face was turning red as his eyes bulged then narrowed at the older man. "I got promoted before a lot of other good cops. Was it your doing?"

Sharp dropped his eyes to the floor and turned his head away. Not looking up at the kid, he said, "You worked hard. You got promoted because you deserved it."

"*Did you influence the decision to make me a detective?*" His voice was a whisper of wrath.

"Lots of guys had recommendations. I put one in for you. And yes, since I can see the question forming, I got you assigned as my partner."

Beyond the screaming fury one might expect, Mitch silently grabbed his coat, curtly nodded to Kahrren, and walked out the door. Sharp jumped up to chase him, but Kahrren's single, firm word stopped him in his tracks. "No." Her hand lifted in an effort to stop him. Unexpectedly, it worked. "He needs some time. This has brought up a lot of stuff for him."

"So I gathered." he pawed at his face and leaned back in the chair, staring up at the ceiling. "But what does this info about Mitch have to do with the murder investigation?"

"I really don't know. But I am anxious to find out."

Chapter Six

Monday
   "No, sir. He doesn't seem to be speaking to me." Sharp explained to Rodriguez in the vaguest terms what transpired on Saturday evening. Mitch had not answered any of Jim's five calls on Sunday.

"Send him to me when he gets here," Rodriguez directed Sharp. "And make sure whatever this is doesn't get in the way of work."

"Yes, sir."

Sharp made his way to his desk and started checking for updates on reports and emails. When Adams rolled in exactly at nine o'clock, he looked up. "Morning. Rodriguez wants to see you." Adams draped his coat over the chair at his desk and without a word to Sharp, turned and headed to speak with Rodriguez.

"Sir, you wanted to see me?"

"Close the door and sit down." His tone was firm and incredibly serious. "I understand there is an issue with you and Sharp."

"Yes, sir. A personal issue. It won't affect my work."

"He said you won't speak to him. How are you going to conduct an investigation without speaking to your partner?"

"I have every intention of speaking to him. About anything work related."

"Adams, I hope whatever this is will be something you can get past. I won't tolerate any bullshit because you're holding a grudge over—whatever this is."

"I'll let you know if I feel the investigation will be affected. I need a little bit of time to work through this issue with Sharp. That's all." Rodriguez nodded, seeming to consider Adams' statement. Adams continued, "I have a question for you, sir."

"What is it?"

"Why did you accept my application to work as a detective under you? Did Sharp have any influence in your decision?"

"He did not. I chose you because of your abilities and your interview." He stopped for a minute to consider. "I did, however, partner you with Sharp at his request."

"Why would you, sir?" Adams's irritability at the statement pulled his face into a grimace.

"Because he is a great detective, despite being an ornery shit. You impressed me with your responses to my questions. I wanted you to have the best training available, which meant pairing you with Sharp. I didn't even ask him why he wanted you. Frankly, I don't care."

Mitch nodded. "Thank you, sir. Will there be anything else?"

"I hope not. Go make some progress. And don't let me hear or see whatever happened between you two is getting in the way." He nodded to the door, excusing Adams and turned back to his paperwork.

Mitch returned to his desk and logged in to his computer. "Any updates on the case?"

Sharp looked at him. "No. We are in the same spot we were on Saturday. Kahrren said she'd call if anything changed on her side." Mitch nodded his understanding and turned his face to the monitor, where he kept it for what seemed to be three eons.

The phone rang and Sharp picked up with a gruff, "Yeah?" He listened for several moments, affirming his understanding with a few grunts and other intonations. He paused to listen for a few moments, then said, "Yep. We'll be over shortly. Yep. Bye."

"Whatcha got?" Adams inquired in a forced professional tone.

"Arnie's got the body out. Said there was some damage from the resin but not enough to stop him from finding results. Wants us to come over and look at what he found."

"Let's do it. I'll tell Rodriguez." Without waiting for a response, he locked his computer, stood, and yanked his coat off the chair as he headed to the boss's office. "Hey, Lieutenant. The M.E. got the body out with minimal damage. He wants us to come see something he found, so we're headed that way."

"Good. Call me as soon as you know something."

The journey to the County Medical Examiner's Office was stone silent. Neither man made an attempt to speak to the other and the tension was strikingly palpable. When they arrived in the parking lot, Sharp shut off the car and turned to speak, but Adams was out of the car as fast as lightning. Following the kid's lead, he got out of the car and headed toward the entry doors. By the time he caught up to Adams, the buzzer had already been pressed and they were waiting to be buzzed in. A few short moments later, they had explained who they were and what their business was, and were allowed access.

They found Sharp's best friend, a very handsome man in a lab coat over scrubs, waiting for them outside the autopsy suites. His sparkling blue eyes floated kindly over a warm, playful smile. "Hello, gentlem— well, Detective Adams and Jim." Dr. Arnold Bauer was a good man, a good friend, and a complete smart ass when it came to dealing with Jim Sharp.

"Ah, shit, Arnie. Don't start already." Sharp was as dour as ever, and it wasn't helped at all by Adams's new policy of avoidance. Adams smiled and nodded at Dr. Bauer's greeting and automatic ribbing of his partner. "You got something to show us, or did you just bring us here to be a dickhead?" Sharp spewed.

"There's some interesting stuff I want to show you about the body. Come with me." Bauer wasn't affected by Sharp's gruffness. He simply ignored it and walked into the suite containing the remains of the formerly encased victim. He waved them in as he led them toward the body. Stopping at the head, he started to explain, "So, I got all the resin off. There was some damage to the muscle tissue, but it's mostly superficial." He pointed to the wrists. "We have evidence of a ligature binding the wrists, as well as something around the neck like a collar. The cause of death was not strangulation though."

Sharp leaned in to observe the marks. "What was it?" Transitioning his gaze to the torso, then continuing upward, he observed multiple incisions on the neck.

Arnie said, "Not sure yet. You can see there are a few cuts on the neck. Those were already there but I haven't had a chance to explore them yet. Neither have I opened him up yet. It's possible my opinion could change entirely once I see what the organs look like." He shrugged.

"Why don't you think it wasn't strangulation?" Sharp asked.

"I don't see damage to the hyoid or any evidence of a garrote." Arnie paused for a moment to allow Sharp to further examine the body. "Additionally there is evidence of some pretty severe damage from repeated sexual battery—anal tearing and rectal fissures at different stages of healing—indicating it was an ongoing occurrence for at least a few days, maybe up to a week."

"Were you able to work out how long it would take to encase him in the plastic stuff?" Sharp was still looking over the body. He looked at Arnie, as he asked the question, then looked at Adams to invite him into the conversation. "Jesus, kid. What the hell is wrong with you?"

Adams's face was bloodless under a layer of sweat. He was panting shallowly and looked to be in an absolute panic. Uncharacteristically, the kid was so wobbly, he started to tip over into a fall. Sharp rushed to him and caught him, then guided him out of the suite, helping him into a chair in the hallway.

"Mitch? Come on, kid. Mitch!" Sharp was gently shaking Adams's shoulder trying to get him to come around, but the kid was unresponsive. Sharp hollered from the hallway, "Arnie? A little help out here?"

Arnie was ahead of Sharp, arriving with a clean, damp towel, and a bottle of water. "Look out, Jim," he said as he stepped between Sharp and Adams. "Detective Adams, I'm going to use this cloth to wipe your face, okay? You'll feel one hand on your shoulder and the other will be in the towel on your face. Here we go." Arnie proceeded exactly as described while Sharp watched from behind, showing concern consistent with a father. "He's okay. His pulse is normalizing, and his eyes are starting to focus. Looks like a panic attack."

Mitch shook his head trying to snap back to full awareness. Looking up at Arnie he said, "I'm okay. Thanks." He took the towel from the doctor and wiped it once more over his forehead before letting it fall to his lap. "That for me?" He pointed to the water bottle which was handed to him.

Sharp stepped forward and took a knee. "Hey, kid. Are you all right? You gave me a good scare there."

"Yeah. I'm fine. It's just… it was a little too familiar, you know?" Mitch's eyes darted up to Arnie's face and back to Sharp. An astute man, Arnie made himself scarce for the moment. "I guess I'll have something to discuss in therapy. Do you mind if I wait outside while you finish up in there? I could use some air."

"Sure. If you think you're okay to walk out, I'll see if there's anything else and meet you back at the car."

"Thanks. I'll be fine."

A few minutes later, Sharp sat down in the driver's seat, seeing how Adams had placed himself as a passenger. "You got the gist of it. He doesn't have anything more at the moment. They're waiting on identification and any other tests to come back."

Adams nodded. "Sorry about all this, Sharp. I've been a little off-kilter and wasn't expecting to see those exact injuries on the vic. *My* exact injuries."

"You wanna take the rest of the day off? I'd understand and so would Rodriguez."

"No. I'll be okay. But if you don't mind stopping at my place, I'd like to change my clothes. I sweated through everything I'm wearing."

"You got it, kid." Sharp pulled into the flow of traffic. "Which way? I just realized I don't actually know where you live."

"Take I-5 North. I have a place on Hayden Island."

Sharp shot the kid a look. "How in the hell can you afford a place up there?" Adams answered with nothing more than a polite lift of the corners of his mouth.

Full cup of coffee in hand, Kahrren headed toward the couch. She leaned to place the cup on a coaster, determined not to spill, when she was startled by a bright and chipper voice belonging to a certain dead girl she knew. "Hiiiiiiieeeeeeee Kaaaahhhrrrreeeeeeeeen!"

"Dammit, Brittany. You could have waited to shout a greeting at me until there was nothing in my hand." The coffee spilled over a large area of the coffee table and was dripping onto the floor. Kahrren was very annoyed.

"What fun would it be?" she grinned.

"You aren't supposed to be having fun. You're supposed to be dead and, I don't know, on some other plane of existence or something." She made her way back to the kitchen to retrieve cleaning products, returning with full hands. "What do you want?"

"I want you to be nice to me." Taking a seat on the chair closest to where the spill occurred, she leaned in and whispered in a breathy sing-song, "Because I know something you don't know." She resumed her typical bubbly tone, "And if *you* want to know, you better change your tune."

Kahrren scowled at the girl and grunted as she knelt on the floor to clean the newly caffeinated carpet. She placed the cleaning supplies on the table and slid onto the couch. "Do you have something to tell me, or shall I call an exorcist?"

"I'm not a demon. And don't be rude."

"Well, it's a matter of opinion as to whether you are or are not, really. Will you *please* tell me what you came to say? I'd like to drink what's left of my coffee in peace."

"I don't think I will, actually. Maybe next time you'll be nice to me, and I'll tell you what I know." After a physical demonstration of the phrase, "Harrumph," Brittany disappeared.

Seizing the opportunity to get a little bit of rest after an exhausting morning at physical therapy, Kahrren kicked up her legs on the reclining chair and sipped her coffee as she enjoyed a serial killer documentary before falling asleep.

Waking to the boom-scuffle of her bestie with boyfriend in tow, her eyes opened, and she thought she proffered words of greeting, though it came out more as a moan. Her face showed a polite smile, so the vocalization was taken as meant.

"Hi, Kahrren. Are you doing okay?" Lorna placed the bags on the floor inside the kitchen door as she waited for a response.

"Mmmhmm," she lowered the footrest of the recliner and shuffled toward the kitchen, collecting her mug and cleaning supplies on the way. In response to Lorna's raised eyebrow, Kahrren offered, "Surprise Brittany visit. She scared me and I spilled my coffee."

"What did she want?"

"She said she had something to say but I *may* have suggested she was a demon and *might* have suggested I was going to call an exorcist, so she had a hissy fit and disappeared."

Flatly, Lorna commented, "How tragic," as she started to put groceries away. "But I hope it wasn't anything important."

Kahrren shrugged. "I guess we'll find out eventually if it is. Here, give me the bag." She reached for the bag Lorna had in hand, but before she could get there, Andrew swooped in and took it. "Hey, I was gonna help," she protested.

"And now I am going to do it." He flashed his playboy smile, cheekily. "Do you need anything before we make dinner?"

"Nothing I can't get for myself, thanks." Her tone was a little sassy, but he seemed to understand the playfulness in it. "What are we having?"

"Well, we couldn't decide between spaghetti or soup and sandwiches. What do you think?" Lorna held up a bag of pasta in one hand and a can of soup in the other.

"It's been cold today. Let's have soup and sandwiches. I can help."

"Nope. We've got it. Go rest. We'll let you know when it's ready." Andrew held out a bottle of water for her, and pushed the door open suggesting her departure.

Kahrren ignored him and looked at Lorna. "He sure got bossy. You helped with this I presume?" She sneered and grumbled as she took the water.

Lorna giggled. "I told him how to handle you. "And how you really like him so he doesn't have to be so careful when he speaks to you, because *you* are a wretched hag who likes to argue."

"You said...*what?*" Kahrren's lower lip rolled forward in a farcical display of injured feelings.

"Yep. Wait until you hear what I say next if you don't get out of my kitchen." Lorna tossed a towel at her friend and returned to unpacking. Kahrren let the towel drop as she blew a raspberry and retreated to her bedroom to visit her other best friend, Fred, a beautiful purple and crimson betta fish.

Her fingers traced the bowl in an affectionate dance with her tiny companion. After a moment, he stopped responding to her travelling digits and started to peck at the surface of the water, indicating it was his dinner time too. She sprinkled a helping of bloodworms into his bowl and watched as he devoured them. The excitement of feeding fish only lasted a few moments, and once passed, she rose and headed to the bathroom to clean up before dinner.

She stepped out of the steamy shower and came face to face with Brittany. Again. Trying her best to maintain her patience, she said, "Hello, Brittany. Back so soon? Is there something I can help you with?"

"No. But there is something I can help you with. I decided you should know what I found out, even if you're mean to me."

"Very magnanimous of you. What is it you'd like to tell me?"

"Well, it seems like there is a connection between the hot detective and the murderer who put the guy in the cube."

This captured Kahrren's interest greatly, as it was precisely what she was picking up when the detectives were here seeking her help. "I'm listening. Please go on."

* * *

As Sharp followed Adams into his home, his eyes were as wide as his mouth was agape. The place was very nice. He never would have guessed the young detective had such elegant taste. "Holy shit, kid. Nice place you've got here."

"Thanks. Make yourself at home." Mitch peeled off his coat and loosened his tie as he headed toward the kitchen. "Want something to drink?"

"Sure. What do you have?"

"I *should* give you kombucha. I know it's your favorite." He grinned, mischievously. "But how about lemonade or tea? I also have water."

"Lemonade sounds great. Thank you." Sharp wandered around the living room, taking in every beautiful and perfectly placed decoration. The house was as well put together as its owner, which meant both were very impressive. "Did you hire someone to decorate?"

"No. I did it myself." He handed Sharp a glass of lemonade, holding another for himself. "Do you like it?"

"It's… astonishing. I never expected your place to look like this." Sharp hesitated. "Don't be offended, but how can you afford this?"

Mitch smiled. "Well, it's really a combination of luck and being frugal. After I was rescued, there were some very nice people who donated money for my care and education. Quite a lot of money, actually. Also, I inherited a bit of money from my grandparents and parents which I invested wisely. I've spent most of my money on my wardrobe and my home, so now, I really only have to pay for utilities and food. So, it works out."

"Christ. You own this outright?"

"Yes. It seemed prudent to buy it outright and not have to pay interest on a home loan." He chugged his lemonade and placed the cup in the dishwasher. "If you don't mind, I'm going to have a quick shower and change. I'll only be a few minutes."

"Yeah, no problem." Sharp continued his perusal of the home while Mitch freshened up. As promised, a short while later the younger detective reappeared, clean and refreshed.

"Okay. I'm all set," he stated, coming from upstairs. "Oh, did you want to see the rest of the house?" His tone was polite, but still very guarded.

"I checked out everything but your bedroom. I tried not to touch anything.

It feels like a museum in here." He chuckled as his hand gestured to the statues and paintings on display. "I'll check out the bedroom some other time. We'd better get going."

"Sure." Mitch grabbed Sharp's glass from its place near the sink and placed it in the dishwasher next to his own. The two headed to the door and left after Mitch set the alarm. "So, where to?"

"Well, back to the station, I suppose." Sharp's awe of his partner's elevated living situation was apparent in his tone and demeanor. "I guess I really don't have to worry about you, eh, kid?"

"You don't need to worry about me. As you can see, *I'm* doing just fine." There was a bit of acid in his tone, though he seemed to be trying to control it.

Sharp winced a little at the slicing statement. "Okay, kid. You've made your point. I'm sorry for interfering. I won't do it again, and I can't do anything more than apologize for what I did before." He paused and waited for a few moments, then said, "So now I am asking for your forgiveness. It's up to you whether you want to hold onto this... whatever this is, or if you want to move past it."

"Don't you *dare* get salty with me. I haven't done anything wrong. I am not the liar or interfering party. I'm doing my best to work through this. It's only been one fucking day, so how's about you cut me a little slack and give me the space to deal with this?" His tone rose from sharp speech to piercing yell as he concluded his statement. Not bothering to wait for a response, he walked away from his partner. As he got in the car, Sharp following a few paces behind, he slammed the door.

As Sharp got into the driver's seat, he muttered, "Ah, hell. That didn't go well," then secured his safety belt and started the car. Another wordless drive passed as they headed back to the precinct.

It was a short appearance at the police station. When Mitch got to his desk, a good thirty seconds ahead of his partner, Lieutenant Rodriguez appeared almost at once. A sticky note adhered to the index finger of his left hand which he extended to the young detective. Adams's already sour face was made even more unpleasant as he tried to read it. "Uhh... help me out, boss.

What is *this* supposed to say?"

"Watch your tone, detective," he warned, in response to the kid's spiciness. "It says you need to talk to the psychic. She wouldn't tell me what her call was about." He nodded as Sharp walked up. "Jim, looks like you guys have a new errand."

"Oh, yeah? What fresh hell is this?" His face squished up as he tried to make out the words on the sticky note held out by Adams.

"The girl called and said she needs to speak to you two. She wouldn't say more."

"The girl?" Sharp asked.

"Kahrren. I'll call her." Mitch handed Sharp the paper as he pulled his phone out of his pocket. "Be right back."

Passing most of the distance of the room and entering the staff lounge, Adams pressed the call button on his mobile. "Hi, Kahrren. It's Mitch Adams returning your call. What can we do for you?"

"Hi Mitch. Are you okay?"

"I'm fine. What do you need?" He was having very little success presenting an amiable tone.

"If it's a bad time we can speak later."

"Kahrren, it's not a bad time, I'm merely not in the mood for chatting or game playing. Can you please tell me how I can help you?"

"Well, I may have a little bit of information regarding your investigation. Would you prefer to speak in person or on the phone?"

"We'll be there shortly." He disconnected without further comment and hastily made his way back toward Sharp. "I'm going over there. Do you want to come?"

"Let's go."

* * *

An aromatic combination of slightly overcooked grilled cheese and canned soup pervaded Kahrren's senses as she answered the call to dinner from the kitchen. Settling in her chair, she said, "This smells great. Thank you."

"You're welcome." Lorna took her seat next to Andrew and set down her plate. "How was therapy today?"

"Exhausting." She dipped the diagonally cut sandwich into the vegetable soup and took a bite. "Mmm. The best way to have vegetables." She looked up and saw Lorna's judgy face, then made a point to swallow, and elaborated, "It wasn't as brutal as before, don't worry. I'm just tired because we did some resistance exercises and some endurance stuff on the treadmill. I have always hated exercise so it was extra sucky."

"First of all, the bits floating in the broth are no longer in a state which could qualify them as vegetables. Secondly, you'd better not push it or I *will* march right back in there and cause a scene."

"Yes, mother," Kahrren responded, purposely talking around a mouthful of food, with the sole purpose of bothering Lorna.

"You are so gross."

A devilish look crossed Kahrren's face. She glanced at Andrew, wondering what his response would be to her next move, then decided she didn't care. She opened her mouth to display a gargantuan portion of partially chewed, soup-soggy sandwich, and made her most grotesque face to match. Lorna was horrified, while Andrew was staring at his soup, lips pressed together and his face turning crimson with effort from trying not to laugh.

"It's no wonder you're single." Lorna rolled her eyes as she took a dainty, ladylike bite of her dinner.

"Oh, *ha-ha!* Any man would be lucky to have me."

"Any man would be saintlike to put up with you, you mean."

"That brings up an interesting question for me, Kahrren." Andrew looked at her inquisitively. "Is your ability the reason you prefer to stay single?"

"It sure is. I have dated here and there, but nothing serious. I can't stand to be in someone's head all the time. It's one thing when it's a friend or coworker, but someone you're supposed to give your heart to? Well, it's a lot tougher not being able to escape knowing how they really feel. I think little white lies or even diplomatically phrased feedback is crucial to a relationship. I don't get those benefits. It's one hundred percent blunt honesty all the time."

"I guess it wouldn't be very romantic, would it?" His posture sagged a little as he looked at her, wearing a clenched half-smile.

"Don't pity me, Andrew. I do all right." She made a saucy little hip swivel implying there were more than a few notches on her headboard, as usual, taking any opportunity to change the mood by being crass.

"I have no doubts. You *are* pretty great. Looks, brains, independence, knowledge of anatomy. What more could a guy ask for?" He looked at Lorna, hoping she wouldn't be upset with flattery aimed at anyone besides her. She was smiling, evidently approving of his assessment.

"You are so sweet, Andrew. I am glad to know you think so highly of my friend."

The two smiled at each other for an intense, emotional moment. "Thank you."

He reached for her hand and squeezed it. The moment was shattered with a retching sound from Little Miss Sunshine. "Get a room."

Her comment was answered by Lorna, whose face was tilted down as she stared up at Kahrren, impatient. Andrew chuckled. They resumed eating and finished as a knock came at the door. Kahrren exclaimed, "Oh, yeah! I forgot to tell you."

"We're having guests?" Lorna grinned, teasing. Andrew rose to answer the door as the two women bantered and headed for the living room.

"Yeah. Brittany came back with her mystery information. I am not sure it will help, but I called Mitch and he said they'd come over. I think he's still in a bit of a mood."

"Oh, marvelous. We needed more snide detective encounters." Lorna plopped on the sofa next to Kahrren, concluding her sassy commentary.

Andrew walked to the sitting area with suit-clad gentlemen in tow and offered them seats in the chairs facing the couch. He quickly grabbed some water bottles from the kitchen, placed them on the table in front of each person, and took his place next to Lorna.

"Nice to see you, gentlemen. Thanks for coming over so quickly." Kahrren was cordial, despite noticing the foul moods of both men.

"Thank you again for your assistance, Kahrren." Sharp reciprocated her politeness. "I understand you have more information you'd like to share?"

"Yes. I believe you should look at the barn where Mitch was kept when he was abducted. It keeps coming up when I touch the resin, and umm…"

"I don't like the sound of that," Sharp responded to her hesitation. "And, umm, what?" He stared at her from behind a wary face, noticeably dreading the answer. He waited another moment as Kahrren and Lorna exchanged glances, while Andrew appeared as baffled as Sharp. Mitch waited silently.

"Well, I haven't told you about something. It's a bit beyond what you know already." She didn't fluster easily, but what she had to say seemed to do the trick. "Well, it's like this… Brittany's ghost has been haunting me since I woke up in the hospital, and she says there is something going on involving the barn."

The room was quiet for what felt forever. "Kahrren, did she say what they should expect to find there?" Lorna attempted to get the conversation moving again, but all of the men sat in unbelieving silence.

Kahrren's black hair slowly grazed her shoulders as she shook her head. "I tried to get her to elaborate but she wouldn't—or couldn't—tell me more. I'm not at all sure which. But if you think about it, it's consistent with what I was picking up from the resin. The boy in the barn."

"You made us come all the way over here for *this?*" Mitch spat. His foul mood was now unmistakable. "This is the same garbage you told us *when you failed* to pick up anything from the resin block, only now you're blaming it on a freaking *ghost?*"

"I didn't *make* you do anything. I asked if you wanted to talk about it on the phone or in person. *You're* the one who decided to bulldoze his way in here without any discussion as to if or when it was convenient. So, don't you dare try to pin it on me."

"Yeah, fine. Do you have anything else to tell us?" He sprang up from his seat in a rage.

"Yeah, how about *go fu—*"

Lorna shot up with her hands flung out trying to stop the exchange, screaming, *"Enough!"* She stood huffing for a minute, interceding on behalf of all involved. "Detective Adams, I can see you're very upset, but it's not Kahrren's fault. If you'd like, we can either continue with Detective Sharp, or do this some other time."

"Talk to Sharp. *I* am so done with this hogwash." He turned and flung the door open, not bothering either to close it behind him, or to wait for his partner.

Sharp, clearly vexed, slowly rose. "Kahrren, thank you very much for the information. If you have anything further, please contact me directly. I'll be grateful for anything you have to offer. And I *apologize* for Detective Adams's behavior." His head rotated back and forth in disbelief as he looked to the door where his partner had so explosively exited. "I am not sure what is going on, but there was no reason for the conversation to go this way. Thank you again for your time." He mashed his lips disapprovingly as he slowly turned and exited.

When Sharp got to the car, it was the only thing waiting for him. His partner had disappeared.

"Well, isn't *that* just perfect?"

Chapter Seven

❦

Wednesday

"No, sir. I haven't heard from him. He never called out?" Sharp's concern for his partner was evident in his tone and demeanor.

"He never called. Not even a text." Rodriguez seemed to teeter between annoyance and concern at the young detective's unscheduled absence. "I know he's been a bit on edge, but I didn't expect a disappearing act."

"I must've called a dozen times. He isn't gonna answer for me. And after the way he blew up at Ms. McClintock, I really couldn't predict what he'll do next. I guess I'll keep working on the case myself." It was as much a statement of intention as a request for permission. "If I head his direction, I'll stop in at the house to see if he's there, and if he's all right.

"Yeah. I'll call him again too. Let me know if you find anything." Rodriguez dismissed the seasoned detective and resumed his duties.

When he returned to his desk, Sharp picked up the receiver as he sat down and tried Adams again. No answer. Next, he sent another text. Still nothing. Heaving a sigh, he set his phone down and fired up his computer.

The new computers recently installed as part of the refurbishment of the station were lightning fast. His inbox indicated receipt of an email. Marked as an important document, he opened an email titled, "Victim Identification Case No. 482027". He took a moment to read the contents, which presented a confirmation of the victim's identity established through dental records. After updating the case notes and checking to make sure the email had been copied to Rodriguez and Adams, he set to work pulling up information on the victim.

Seeing no notable correlations to other cases, Sharp continued his review of all of the case's facts. Again. This case was getting cold, fast.

As lunchtime approached, he made the decision to visit the family of the victim to notify them of their loved one's passing. He rose and walked to Rodriguez's open door, leaning in. "I'm going to take care of the notification, then get some lunch and drive up to the kid's place, to check it out, if that's all right with you."

"Keep me posted," he assented.

Two and half hours later, Sharp texted Rodriguez: No one at his house. Car gone. Will keep trying.

* * *

The Columbia River was gray and lazy under the low cloud cover. Rain had been pouring down all day, but it didn't stop Mitch from making the decision to go for a hike. His need to clear his head superseded any concern over weather conditions. A little rain wasn't going to deter a native Portlander. *And it's never as bad as they say it's going to be.*

Being an avid fitness enthusiast, he had athletic gear for any condition. Outfitted in warm and water repellent hiking gear, he headed south, up the hill toward Coopey Falls, just a short drive from Portland.

The falling water was always pretty, but he spent virtually no time standing in awe of its pulchritude. Feeling the need to burn off the aggression and anger which had so frequently been peeking up to the surface lately, he ditched any semblance of a trail as he passed the flat area, which had been cleared of rock and trees, and now served as a common stopping point to take in the view. Paying no attention to the rugged terrain of broken, scattered rocks and gnarled tree roots under camouflaging ferns, he tore through the landscape with fierce determination.

Hours of climbing aimlessly had taken their toll, and he sat, pulling food and water from his pack. His breathing was still labored from the constant exertion he'd forced his way through. Once calmed, he sank his teeth into a variety of healthy, but high calorie snacks. He'd need the fuel to continue the abuse of his body, as he planned to continue through the wilderness.

Miles away from his starting point, he closed his eyes, quietly taking in the hiss of the rain hitting the varying surfaces of the forest. His surroundings were entirely serene, a stark contrast to the landscape of his mind. The past few days had been an unexpected struggle for him and made no promise of remedy.

He mulled over the series of ordeals he'd experienced in the last few days. His partner's betrayal, seeing the corpse with wounds he had experienced himself as a child, blowing up at the massage therapist, each making the last feel sharper and more hurtful in a cyclical emotional clusterfuck. He lowered his face into his hands as his breathing deepened. The next thing he knew he was weeping. He wept until he sobbed, then he sobbed until his body fell over in exhausted surrender. He lay under a gray sky, on the reasonably flat rock he had perched upon to eat lunch. There was a short reprieve in the rain, leaving behind a cloud layer, hiding him from the sun.

His emotional turmoil faded into exhaustion, then transitioned into a serenity typically found when there are no more tears to be cried. He started to drift into unconsciousness, but startled as he heard the crunch of broken branches only steps from him. Attempting to turn to locate the source of the noise, he pushed himself up with one arm in an effort to turn far enough to see. All he saw was a blur of black clothing and a flash of light as his head was bashed by something hard.

* * *

Thursday

The headboard knocked hard into the wall as Kahrren bolted upright screaming in her sleep.

The agonized shrieks of her best friend launched Lorna out of bed, toward Kahrren's room. She threw the door open and ran to the bed. When she reached Kahrren, she grasped her by the shoulders and tried to gently shake her into awareness.

The agonized shrieks died and were replaced by a deep gasp and wide eyes as Kahrren came sharply back to consciousness and looked around. Pulling her knees to her chest, she began to sob in relief when she looked around and saw she was in the safety of her room. Lorna's arms slipped around her shoulders and pulled her into an embrace.

Andrew appeared a few minutes later with two cups of tea. Setting them down, he asked Lorna, "Is she okay?"

Lorna nodded. "I think she will be okay. I haven't been able to get her to say anything yet." She looked up at him with wet eyes, and said with a shaky voice, "It must have been a bad dream." The head resting on her shoulder started slowly shaking back and forth.

"I need my phone." Kahrren pushed herself with one arm into a sitting position. She gently pulled away from Lorna. "I think it was more than a dream." She reached to her nightstand to retrieve her phone.

"What do you mean?" Lorna's eyes searched Kahrren's face. She left her hand on Kahrren's shoulder, as much to comfort herself as her friend. "More than a dream?"

"I really only want to say this once, if you don't mind, so I'm calling Sharp, and you can stay and listen." She held her phone in her left hand as she picked up the mug of tea and lifted it Andrew's direction and nodded. After sipping the scorching beverage, she returned it to the nightstand. Lifting her phone she started to flip through the contacts on her phone until she found her query and hit the send button.

"This better be good," the gravelly voice sniped from the other end of the line.

"Detective Sharp, it's Kahrren. I think Mitch is in trouble."

71

"Have you heard from him? What did he say?"

"Not exactly. I think I had a vision."

"You *think* you had a vision?"

"I was sleeping. At first it felt like a nightmare, but it changed. It was intense. I saw him getting hit in the head. I sensed how scared he is—like panicking. I don't know where he is, but he's in the dark. His head hurts and it's pitch black." Kahrren struggled to fill her lungs.

"Have you tried calling him? He hasn't been picking up for me."

"Not since our...disagreement."

"Thank you, Kahrren. Please let me know if you pick up anything else. I'll keep you updated." The line disconnected but wasting no time, Kahrren found Mitch's number in her contacts and tapped to start the call. She tapped her foot furiously as she waited for the line to pick up, but she only got voicemail. She tossed her phone down on the bed. "I'm so sorry for waking you."

"Oh, Kahrren..." Lorna's soft voice was as warm as her embrace. "You don't have to be sorry. I'm glad you're okay. Well, relatively speaking." She sipped her tea. "Do you think we should call Bub?"

"Yes. He'll be furious if I don't call him."

* * *

The darkness shrouding Mitch's house was suffocating. After pounding on the door and yelling his partner's name for the better part of ten minutes, Sharp started looking in the windows. The absence of light and movement weighed heavily on Sharp's chest. His shouts became faster and higher in pitch. He jumped when his phone rang. "Sharp."

"It's Rodriguez. I received a call from the chief about Adams. He said Ms. McClintock called after having a vision. Have you reached him yet?"

"She called me too. I'm at his house right now. I've been pounding for ten minutes and yelling his name but it's dark and I don't see his car. I am pretty sure he isn't here."

"Did she give you any details?"

"She said she thinks he's hurt and afraid. And it's dark where he is."

"How badly hurt?"

"I'm not sure. She said he was hit in the head. She woke me up, so I didn't think to ask. I jumped directly into the car and came here. Are you at the station?"

"Not yet but I am heading there now. So is the chief. If you're done I want you there too."

"On my way." Sharp disconnected and started back toward his car. He stopped and turned back to the window, reaching into his pocket for his phone. He dialed the kid again and peeked in the window. He saw the flashing light of a cell phone on the kitchen counter. "Son of a bitch."

* * *

"Boo!" Brittany clearly thought she was being funny when she popped up next to Kahrren at the kitchen table. Had she taken time to read the room before her little joke, she'd have seen that none present were in a jovial mood. "Jeez, what's wrong with all of you?"

Oblivious to the appearance of the spectre, Andrew and Lorna continued sipping their tea and snacking on cookies. Kahrren scowled at what to them appeared to be an empty chair.

"Brittany's here. She thinks she's funny." Because of the way her head tilted forward leaning on her hand, her sideways look toward the lovebirds appeared as an eyeroll, though it wasn't. "And clearly they don't have timekeeping devices on the other side because it's the *middle of the night.*" The clock read 3:27 a.m.

"I come in the middle of the night all the time. Only, you don't know about it." She flashed her best disturbing grin and wiggled her eyebrows.

Who knew dead people could be so creepy? "Okay, first of all, stop coming here in the middle of the night. That's just wrong," she said to Brittany.

"She's really here right now? Does she know where Mitch is?" Lorna's speech was fast and hopeful.

"Yes, she's really here," she said to Lorna, then turned toward the vacant chair. "Brittany, do you know anything about where Mitch is? He's gone missing."

"Missing? No. I was…somewhere else."

"Can you please try to find him? Do you know any more than you told us before?"

"I'll see what I can find out. I don't know anything for certain. I'll be back." She disappeared before Kahrren could question her further.

* * *

The doors swung closed behind Sharp as he hoofed it into the police station. The office was eerily quiet at this time of the morning. His soggy footprints trailed behind him from the cascades of rain which had again begun falling.

He crossed the threshold into Rodriguez's office to find no one there. He turned on his heel and headed straight for Adams's desk. Every drawer was a dead end, every file was bereft of helpful information. He slammed the last cabinet closed and swore.

Lieutenant Rodriguez entered the open space accompanied by Chief Donovan. "Sharp, what do we know? Catch the chief up," he barked as he entered his office followed by the other two.

"Adams has been disturbed by a number of things lately. My interference in his career, the fact that I know his background, similar injuries on the victim to what he experienced as a child. Also, Ms. McClintock's assertion that this case we've been working on is somehow related to him."

Donovan responded, "What do you mean similar injuries?"

"Sir, I don't know if you're aware, but Mitch Adams is the boy in the barn."

Donovan's eyes nearly popped out of his head. He looked at Rodriguez. "You didn't tell me that."

"I didn't think it was relevant, sir. It's not something anyone really wants to talk about." Rodriguez commented.

"Is that why Kahrren is involved in this? She knows about his background?"

There was a brief pause as the men decided who would speak next. Sharp decided he'd take this one. "Sir, are you aware when Alex McClintock found the boy in the barn it was because his daughter told him where he was being held?"

"I have been made aware of the fact, yes."

"Well, I was there too. Adams didn't know it until recently. I was there when they found him. I had been assigned McClintock as my first partner when I made detective. After the whole thing happened, I made sure he had everything he needed growing up, but I never told him about it."

"And so?"

"It included recommending him when he was trying to become a detective. Hell, even when he applied to the academy. He only found out a few days ago and has been having a hard time trying to wrap his head around the fact that he may not have gotten to where he is on his own." He swallowed and shook his head. "Then the guy who kidnapped and abused him as a kid was let out of prison. We went to see this crazy cube body and speak with the medical examiner. He had a panic attack when he saw the evidence of restraints and sexual abuse. Those were the same injuries he suffered as a child. Then Kahrren told him she thought this case was related to his own abduction and he blew up."

"And disappeared?" Donovan asked.

"Yes, sir."

"And has my goddaughter given you any helpful information? What has she told you exactly?"

"When we were there she said the case was related, which seemed unlikely at the time." His face paled. "She said check the barn. But it was before Mitch had disappeared. We need to check the barn."

Chief Donovan's cell phone rang. He hit the talk button and commanded, "Go."

The phone on Rodriguez's desk rang two seconds later. "Yeah?" he answered.

A rapid succession of firm orders spewed from each of the men. Donovan ended his call first. "We may not make it to the barn for a while. There's flooding on the highway on the Washington side of the river, and a mudslide on the freeway on our side. There are a lot of people they have to rescue. The fire department is heading out and our guys are going to help with traffic and crowds, if there are any. And this rain is supposed to get much worse tonight."

Rodriguez cradled the receiver. "We've got a body. I'll call Det—" His phone rang again. He picked up and listened after grunting his name. He hung up and looked at Sharp. "We can't get to the body because more streets are flooding. They said it's a real mess out there. Keep your phone on. I'll let you know when you can get there."

Sharp stepped out of the office and closed the door, but was called back by Rodriguez.

"Yes, sir?"

"Check with the parole officer for the guy who kidnapped Adams as a kid. Make sure he's been where he's supposed to be."

Sharp nodded his understanding and stepped out again. After he closed the door, he rubbed his hand over his face. He stood for a moment, his throat thick and his stomach churning. *That son of a bitch better not be involved.*

* * *

The sky lightened enough behind the clouds to indicate dawn had come. Kahrren fell asleep on the couch when Lorna and Andrew found their way back to the bedroom for a few hours of sleep, but the screeching alarm clock put the brief solace to an end.

Lorna carried a mug of coffee out of the kitchen and sat in a chair in the living room to watch the news. The newscaster looked grim as he stated, "If possible, residents of Portland should stay home. Roads are treacherous and there are dozens of road closures due to mud and rock slides from the torrential downpour over the city early this morning. Traffic is backed up all over the city. Rescue crews are working diligently to assist those affected."

"It's a mess out there," Kahrren croaked, rubbing her eyes.

"So it seems. I guess we'll be working from home today." Lorna procured another cup of joe from the kitchen and headed toward her bedroom to share the news.

A short while later Andrew and Lorna set up a workstation at the kitchen table. Their pleasant chatter and usually innocuous sounding keyboard tapping were more than Kahrren's pounding head could take so she headed back to her bedroom. She made a quick call to Thrive to let them know she would not be coming to therapy because of the weather conditions, then slid into her bed and put on her noise canceling headphones. She selected a gentle guided meditation to lull herself back to sleep, which after the horrific and exhausting episode she experienced during the night, did not take long.

The cuffs around her wrists and ankles were so tight, they made her hands and feet cold and tingly. Her limbs were pulled so far away from her prone, naked torso, she could barely manage a wiggle, much less any attempt at escape. She could see an impression of a shadow on the wall from under the blindfold as it slid just up far enough to peek under. Her head was pounding so hard it made her whole body tense. She felt a hand on her hip as she realized someone was behind her on the mattress, and what that touch meant.

She gasped loudly as she sat up in her own bed, tearing at her head to remove the headphones as sheets and blankets fell to the floor in an attempt to free herself from any kind of restriction. She rose as quickly as she could and headed into the bathroom. The water felt cool as she splashed her face and filled her mouth, trying to wash away the sleep, and more importantly, the dream.

She returned to her bed and sat on the edge. Her iPhone felt warm to the touch as she took it off the charger and dialed. "Detective Sharp? I really think you need to look at the barn."

"Ms. McClintock, are you all right? You sound a little rough."

"I'll be fine. I think I had a vision about Mitch. In my sleep again."

"Is he alive?"

"Yes. But he is definitely not okay…" She waited for a moment, but it seemed Sharp was expecting her to elaborate. "I think he's tied up with straps of some kind. And… well, like when he was a kid. Blindfolded. And… well, the rest."

"Are you sure about this? About him being held against his will?"

"As sure as I have ever been."

"Thank you. Let me know if you get anything else. The roads are flooded but I'm going up there as soon as the road is passable." He disconnected and the line went silent.

Kahrren rose and went to the kitchen. She poured some coffee and turned toward the table. "Mitch is in big trouble. Like when he was a kid."

Lorna's eyes bugged out when she laid them on her friend. "What the hell? You are so pale. Come sit down." She popped up from her chair and assisted Kahrren to a seat. "Where is your cane?"

"I forgot it. I'm fine." After a sip of her coffee she set it down and reached for a napkin and a piece of cinnamon roll of highly questionable quality, placing it in front of her, only to stare at it. "I think Mitch *is* in the barn and he is being…"

"Hurt?" Lorna offered a word which showed she understood not only what was meant, but that talking about it was difficult.

Kahrren nodded and her eyes got glassy as she picked at the grocery store pastry, never attempting to take a bite. "But with the roads like this, they can't get out there to look for him."

"How do you know?" Andrew asked, closing the laptop to offer his full attention.

"I had another vision. I called Sharp to tell him and he said so."

"Man, what a rough night. Can Lorna or I do anything for you?"

Kahrren shook her head and rubbed her slightly sticky fingers on the napkin. "You're a good man, Andrew. I appreciate it."

"Jesus, you must be in bad shape. You never hand out compliments."

Kahrren managed to crack a smile and her shoulders quickly rose and fell as they would when laughing. "I'll caffeinate and get back to my regularly scheduled program."

They shared a smile and Kahrren went back to picking at her food. "Where on Earth did you get this monstrosity? Is it edible?" One side of her upper lip rose, following her one-sided nostril flare and squint. "I mean, yuck."

"You'd prefer something else, Your Highness?" Lorna grinned, playfully.

"Nah. I'll stick with this." She raised her mug and continued drinking.

* * *

Sharp's chin rested on his hand as his body slumped forward over his desk. Dark circles and enough bags to open a luggage shop seemed to hold up his drooping eyelids. He read over the same lines of the same document about a thousand times and still didn't comprehend what it was saying.

The call he'd made to the parole officer was not fruitful, with a report that Keres had obtained and been attending work, as well as showing up for the meetings scheduled with his parole officer. Feeling helpless was not a look Sharp wore well.

"Go home. Get some sleep." Rodriguez barked the order at him as he passed by, looking less than exceptional, himself. "I'll call you when there is something you can do."

"No. I—"

"*Go!* You're no good to anyone like this. I'm not asking."

The rubor of anger colored his cheeks. There wasn't a damn thing he could do about it. "Fine."

The normally twenty minute drive to his house in Northeast Portland took over an hour with the state of the roads. Passing over his threshold, he peeled off his soaking wet jacket and dried it with a towel he kept on the coat rack, for just such an occasion. It *was* leather, after all.

After half a leftover sandwich and a quick but scorching shower the old cuss fell unconscious in his bed.

Pouring rain pounded on the roof and windows as he roused in the early afternoon. He dressed, ate, drank some coffee, and tidied up a bit. His house was generally pretty clean, being as he was the only one living there, and he spent most of his time at work.

He reached for his phone which had no alerts of any kind. "Damn." He pressed the button to turn on the television and flipped to the local news. "Aaah, come *on!* When are they gonna get these damn roads clear?" Throwing his body back against the pillow, he impatiently watched the news and waited for the phone to ring. Minutes turned to hours before he had an idea.

His coat felt dry but cool as he slipped into it and grabbed his keys. It was barely above freezing when he got in his car. He fired up the engine and pulled away, heading northeast. His wipers were on double time as he traversed the city, and he still couldn't see *shit*.

* * *

Kahrren was snacking on potato chips and onion dip when an excited knock pulled her attention from yet another serial killer documentary. She lifted herself out of the chair but was beat to the door by Lorna. When the diminutive blonde pulled the door open, both women were surprised to see a hopeful Detective Sharp.

Sharp's brows raised asking for permission from Lorna to enter. She ushered him in with the swing of her arm and stood out of his way. "Ms. McClintock, you got a minute?"

"Uh, yeah. But I wasn't expecting you." She looked down at her mismatched pajamas, featuring a variety of cacti on her pants over a light green background and a ragged vintage t-shirt with the faded face of Jimi Hendrix. Sharp chuckled as he took in her outfit. "Not a word," she said.

Shaking his head and averting his eyes in acceptance of her last directive, he walked in and found a place in a chair facing the couch. "I had a really interesting idea. You wanna go for a ride with me?"

"Give me two seconds." She bolted back to her bedroom, which is to say, though she was rushing, she only *nearly* approached the speed of an average person. She brushed her teeth and hair, which she threw into a quick ponytail, and dressed quickly in a long sleeved black shirt under her favorite dark gray Nirvana tee, and black leggings. "Where are we going?" she asked as she slipped her sock covered feet into gray waterproof boots.

Lorna protested, "Um, it's a disaster out there. Where in the hell are you taking her?" She stood in front of him placing her arms haughtily on her hips. "They are saying the roads are a mess and there's another wave of the storm coming. I don't think you should be going anywhere."

Kahrren kissed Lorna's cheek. "I'll be fine. I'm gonna be with a cop. And I have my phone. Let's go, Sharp. I like this idea."

The detective shot her a conspiratorial smile and plowed ahead through the still open door. Wrapping her scarf around her neck, she walked toward the door, raincoat under her arm, cane in hand. "Bye, Mom. I'll be home for dinner!" She stuck her tongue out at the tiny blonde stomping her foot in the foyer and closed the door.

Chapter Eight

"I guess you don't need to hear my plan?" Sharp glanced at Kahrren once they were situated in the car.

"Nah, I just had to ask you to get your thoughts going that direction."

Sharp whipped out his phone and hit the send button. "Arnie? Incoming." He looked at Kahrren and smirked. "And I'm bringing a friend." After disconnecting, he tossed his phone in the center console. "Have you ever tried anything like this before?"

"Nope. Never had occasion to. What made you think of this?"

"I was at home waiting for a call from my boss to say the roads were clear so I can go up to the barn to look for Mitch, but things seem to be going from bad to worse on that front. I started going over this cube case in my mind and it dawned on me, if you can pick up stuff through touch, why not have you touch the actual victim to see what you get? It seems like an obvious course of action, right?"

"Well, I guess so. I never really thought of it. I don't really spend my days dreaming of fondling corpses."

"You're twisted," he chuckled. "But maybe you should have."

Kahrren's teeth flashed in a grimace and her head pulled back. "That's kinda morbid, don't you think?"

He shrugged. "It's not the worst it's gonna get today, so buckle up." His brows wiggled in a manner reminiscent of Groucho Marx. She shook her head and snorted.

When they pulled into the parking lot at the Medical Examiner's office, they parked right next to the door. The parking lot was empty save for their dark blue sedan and Arnie's silver Mercedes. They exited the car and hustled to reach the cover of the overhang protecting the area in front of the door. Sharp pressed the button and a buzzer sounded. He opened the door and motioned for Kahrren to enter and followed her in.

"Hiya, Jim. How is it out there?"

"Awful and getting worse."

"Who is this young lady?" Though his question was aimed at Sharp, his attention quickly moved to Kahrren. He reached out his hand to shake. "I'm Dr. Arnold Bauer." Arnie smiled politely, his crystal blue eyes sparkling warmly.

"I'm Kahrren McClintock. It's nice to meet you."

"And you. How may I help you?" His face brightened as he waited for her response.

"Kahrren's here to help me with the investigation of the body in the cube, Arnie. Can we see the victim?"

"Oh, you don't want her to see that, do you?" The pitch of his voice dropped, and his head shook back and forth.

"I'm afraid so. She is acting as a consultant for me, and we need to get in there."

"What kind of consultant?"

"Uhh—"

"I'm a psychic," Kahrren jumped in when Sharp began to sputter. "Yes, it's true. No, we're not pulling your leg. Yes, he probably has lost his mind." She glanced at the detective whose mouth had fallen open and was looking a bit dazed. When she looked back at Dr. Bauer, his expression mirrored Sharp's. "Now, if you please, may we go back there? I don't want to hang around here any longer than I have to." She shot Sharp a look hoping he'd understood. *There is some freaky shit happening in this place.*

Arnie stood silent for a moment. He slowly began to shake his head, then shrugged. "Well, okay. I can see there is some stuff going on here I'm not aware of. I'll take you at your word that this is a good idea, despite my better judgment." To Sharp, he directed, "Is she going to have an adverse reaction like your partner?"

"I don't think so, but Ms. McClintock isn't very predictable."

Kahrren gave Sharp the stink eye as the trio turned toward the autopsy suites. By the time Kahrren was setting foot over the threshold of the room containing the body from the cube, her fingers were massaging her temples and her eyes were half closed. She steadied herself on her cane, then proceeded to the center of the room, where stood a silver table.

Sharp's earlier call had given Arnie ample time to retrieve the victim from refrigerated storage, and the remains were waiting for her, covered by a white evidence sheet. Pulling the sheet back, Arnie said to Sharp, "Did you get my report this morning?"

"No. You figure something out?"

"Well, I finished the autopsy last night. It appears this man was still alive when whoever did this started the process. The tox screen showed a near-fatal level of heroin so he would have been unconscious in seconds, but in my opinion it's more likely he died from exsanguination."

"Come again?" Sharp blinked rapidly as his head tilted.

"He made an incision here above the clavicle. He inserted a tube and pumped the fluid in through the carotid artery, and as it pushed the blood through the body, it came back and drained from the severed jugular vein." He pulled the incision slightly apart with his gloved hand to demonstrate. "The red blood cells would rupture with such an injection, but since his blood was being drained as formaldehyde was pumping in, it probably didn't happen fast enough to kill him. This guy didn't have a chance. He could have died of multiple organ failure due to acidosis but that likely would have taken longer as well. The formaldehyde would damage any type of tissue in the body and eventually make the blood so acidic everything would stop."

Sharp wanted to make sure he understood. Who could believe such a thing? "He was embalmed alive?"

Dr. Bauer nodded, looking grim.

"Sharp? I can't stay here much longer. I'm starting to feel... unwell."

Kahrren gripped the edge of the table, her normally pale skin turning ghostly. "Let's do this."

"Are you sure you're up to this?"

"Yes. If we do it now."

Arnie interjected, "What is she going to do?" He looked from Sharp to Kahrren. "Christ, Jim, she looks terrible."

"Can you get her a chair? I think we may need it."

Arnie scrambled to the hallway to find a seat for the young woman. Once he was through the door she reached her hand out. As her warm fingers contacted the victim's cold chest, her eyes grew wide, and she emitted the most blood-curdling scream the men had ever heard. She screamed, "*No!*" in a protracted, agonized, deep moan that seemed other-worldly.

Sharp caught her as she lost consciousness, lowering her to the floor as he grunted from the exertion.

When Kahrren awoke she was lying on the floor, staring up at the lights of a morgue. *Well, this is disconcerting.*

"Are you okay, kid?" Sharp was kneeling next to her and leaned over her, much too close to her face for comfort.

She grimaced and said, "I will be once you get your big melon head out of my face. It's called personal space. You should look into it."

Sharp sat back on his heels and grinned. "She's being a smart ass. She's fine."

"Jim, if you bring one more of these sensitive people here, I am gonna kick your ass into next week." Arnie plopped down in the chair he'd procured for Kahrren. Lifting his hand to cover his eyes, he gave a long, profane sigh. "*Shit.*" He extended his foot and playfully kicked Jim right in the ass.

Jim waved him off with a smirk and turned to Kahrren. "Are you ready to get up?"

She nodded and held her hand out for assistance. "Thanks."

Arnie jumped up and assisted Sharp in getting Kahrren to the chair. His medical training seemed to be paying off for the people Jim was bringing into his office. "How are you feeling? Dizzy? Nauseated?"

"A little of both, but it's not bad. I'm fine."

He reached gently to her neck and as their eyes met she tilted her head slightly back and to the right giving him permission to check her vitals. "Huh. Weird. I expected your pulse to be slower but it's rather elevated."

"Yeah, I don't really like it here. And I was nearly strangled to death in March, so just letting you check my pulse was... unpleasant."

"I'm so sorry. I didn't know."

"Of course you didn't. I know you didn't mean me any harm. But I thank you for waiting for my permission." She lifted the corner of her mouth politely, unable to muster a real smile.

His hand came to rest gently on her shoulder as the corner of his mouth mimicked hers in lifting. He leaned to look closely at her eyes and then leaned back to examine her overall appearance. "I think you'll be all right. But if you feel like you're going to pass out again, do it somewhere else." Every one of his teeth showed in a cartoonish, evil grin. He turned to Sharp. "Dinner tonight? The wife's expecting you."

"There's a chance I may not make it. We are waiting for the roads to be cleared to be able to get to a... new case."

"Call when you know. Did you get what you needed?"

Sharp looked at Kahrren questioningly.

"I think we got as much as we are going to get." She proffered an unclear answer, planning to tell Sharp what happened once they got to the car. "Thank you, Dr. Bauer."

"Call me Arnie, young lady. Feel better." He lazily raised his hand in Sharp's direction. "See you later, you miserable bastard."

"Lucky me," Sharp responded, sarcastically.

Sharp held the door for Kahrren to get in the car, handed her the seatbelt, and closed the door. Once he secured himself in his own seat he turned to her. "What did you see?"

"Sweet Jesus. Do you know anything about the victim? Was he a bad guy?"

"Not as far as we have been able to tell. By all accounts and all records we could find, he was squeaky clean."

She frowned. "Well, I'm not entirely sure what it was, then. I've never seen anything like it." She heaved a sigh, fighting back tears once again. "It was the scariest thing I've ever experienced in my entire life." She turned to him. "It was kind of like when I saw Sarah Donis die, only much, much worse. I think I was actually dying. When I saw the vision from Donis's killer, I could feel her life leaving. In there, my own life was not really slipping away, but actively being pulled from me. Something grabbed my soul and was trying to take it from me."

"In my thirty-something years as a police officer, I've never heard of such a thing." His jaw fell slack and he ran his hand through his hair. "But I've also never encountered anyone like you. And I hope like hell I never do again."

"Ha!" Her monosyllabic guffaw was loud and genuine. Since his visit to her hospital room in the spring when she had confided in him about the increase of her abilities, she had really come to like the man. "Well, it's not very likely, so I think you're probably in luck." A brief moment passed in silence. "I'm pretty sure if I try that again, I'll die." Her lower lip quivered in an uncharacteristic show of emotional vulnerability. Her raspy voice squeaked as she continued, "And I don't want to die."

Sharp reached out and placed his hand gently on her knee, in his best paternal gesture. She grasped it and squeezed as her body shook with sobs.

* * *

That evening when she arrived home, Kahrren plopped down on the couch. Dark circles and puffiness made her look nearly as bad as she felt. She didn't have it in her to yell, so she pulled her phone out and texted Lorna to let her know she'd returned home safely. A few short minutes later, the pajama-clad woman bounced into the living room, a fiery look on her face. "It's about time. It's almost nine o'clock!"

"Sorry. I didn't think we'd be gone so long. It took a little while to do what we went for, then I needed a rest, and we stopped to get something to eat. The apocalypse is happening outside but there's always a fast food place open."

"Okay, well, if you're still hungry, there's food for you in the fridge." She seated herself across from Kahrren. "So, where did you go?"

"You're not gonna like it."

"I already don't like it, but you look atrocious, so I am very curious."

"We went to the morgue so I could touch the body."

"And how did it go?"

"Well, I won't be doing it again. Touching corpses... bad."

"Something happened, didn't it?"

"That's another reason why we took a while. I had to tell Sharp what I saw. After I passed out in the medical examiner's office and had a meltdown in the car. It was totally embarrassing." She looked at Lorna's face and saw a look she knew well. It was impatience. "If you want a drink, better get it now. We'll be here for a few."

"I'm fine. Proceed."

"Oooh, you're spicy this evening!"

"I don't like it when you do stupid, dangerous crap like this."

"Well, it won't happen again, I promise. First of all there was a lot of *activity* at the ME's office. People were trying to come to terms with their deaths. It was bizarre because I could hear a bunch of voices, but thankfully I didn't see anything. Then I went in to touch the body. Oh, man. Sharp said the victim seemed like a good guy, but I don't think so. I saw a lot of bad stuff he never got caught for. He was a rapist. I saw three attacks before it changed. I saw Enoch Keres. You know who he is, right?"

"That's the guy who attacked Mitch?"

"Yes. Well, evidently Keres wanted to revisit the site where he held Mitch because he was out near the barn when he caught this guy raping a woman out there. It was so brutal. He left the woman out there in really bad shape and put this guy in the trunk of his car. He drugged him, held him captive and abused him, much the same way he did to Mitch. After a while he decided to kill him. He gave him a ton of drugs and started the embalming process while the guy was still alive. I didn't tell Sharp or Dr. Bauer, the medical examiner, but I think the guy was aware of what was happening, even though he was unconscious. I felt some real anger about his death."

"Embalmed alive?"

"Horrible, right? But it gets worse…"

"Oh, boy, here we go."

"You're not joking. This is the reason I will *never* touch another corpse again. When I was touching him, something grabbed me. I guess I'd say it grabbed on to my soul. And it tried to take me down with it. It tried to kill me. I don't know if it was his spirit or something else entirely, but—"

"But you almost died again." There was no question in what she said. Her eyes cast downward and she shook her head. "Can we please take a break from you almost dying? I mean, isn't it someone else's turn now?"

"Hopefully someone we don't know. But please don't be mad. It's not like I knew I was going to be in danger. I don't have any way of knowing what will happen with my abilities until I try to use them."

"But now you know?"

"Yes. Now I know and I promise you, I am out of the corpse fondling business."

"Do you want your food?" Evidently, shoving Kahrren full of food was Lorna's love language.

"What is it?"

Lorna smiled and walked to the kitchen. A few minutes later she brought a nuked portion of scalloped potatoes and some pizza rolls.

"Aww, comfort food! You know exactly what I need."

"I figured whatever you were up to would be hard and you might need it." She put her hand on Kahrren's arm and squeezed.

* * *

As Sharp pulled away from dropping Kahrren off, his phone rang. The roads leading to the murder scene were clear but they were still working on the roads through the Columbia River Gorge.

"You'll be meeting up with Detective Daniels since you're short a partner." Rodriguez provided Sharp the address to the crime scene. "He's already on the way."

"Oh, good. The fun never stops." Sharp sighed. "That'll be fine, sir. I'm heading there now."

"Something you want to get off your chest, Detective?"

"No, sir. I'm just wound up about Mitch, and there's always another murder."

"That's the nature of the beast, I'm afraid." Rodriguez disconnected.

Sharp parked on the street outside the destination. It was a rough area of duplexes and run-down apartments off the 99W, which despite its misleading designation, ran north and south. The housing units were tucked behind an industrial area, hiding behind a warehouse for production lighting and a gas station.

Onlookers were standing around the area, trying to catch a glimpse of the body. "You guys know anything about what happened?" They all shook their heads. "Don't you have anything better to do?" Sharp growled an order for them to back up. "If these people have nothing to contribute, get 'em out of here!" he yelled at the closest uniformed cop. The people scrambled.

He headed up the steps to find his temporary partner. The man had light brown hair and was in his early forties. He was shorter than an average man with a slim, wiry build. Sharp nodded as he approached. "What have we got?"

"Hey, Sharp. Nice to see you, man." He turned his attention to this gunshot victim lying on the floor of the kitchen. "GSW to the chest. Reports of shouting before the shot, and someone fleeing on foot immediately following the sound of the blast." He lifted his chin and peered toward the baking dish on the stovetop. "Too bad for this guy. Whatever this was supposed to be actually smells pretty good."

"Oh, yeah. Blood and casserole. My favorite." Sharp smirked at the man, and the two went to work.

Kahrren meandered into the kitchen on Saturday morning to find Andrew had already gone out into the world to procure breakfast. Two half-full coffee cups were on the kitchen counter next to a full one with her name written on it. She flipped open the pink pastry box and widened her eyes as her mouth started to water. There was a donut with chocolate frosting *and* chocolate chips. "My favorite!" she said to herself.

"Do you *always* talk to yourself when you're alone? You're kinda weird."

Kahrren didn't think anyone else was home, and technically she was right. Andrew and Lorna were, in fact, out running an errand. The young woman before her was none other than the bobble-headed Brittany. "Do you always have to scare me?"

"No, but I sure do enjoy it."

Kahrren swiped her hand through the air, directly through where Brittany's abdomen would have been were she still alive.

"Hey! Stop it!"

"From now on, every time you scare me, you're getting swiped."

"Jeez. Drink your coffee. You're grumpy."

"I *wasn't* until you scared me. I was quite happy when I woke up to find there were donuts." She glanced into the box to explore further. "Ooh, looks like scones, bagels, and muffins too. God, I love carbs." She picked up the death-by-chocolate donut and took a monster bite. She was halfway done chewing when she asked, "Do you have news?"

"Well, you definitely need to send the old grumpy cop to the barn if he wants to find his partner. He's there. But he's not looking so hot."

"Shit."

"And I think sooner is better than later. I don't like the look of the hole being dug outside. Luckily it keeps getting washed out and filled with mud from the rain. But I'd recommend he hurry."

"Thank you, Brittany." Kahrren took a sip of her coffee and set it on the counter next to her donut. She flashed the girl a wicked grin and said, "Help yourself," as she walked out of the kitchen feeling superior and chuckling at her own joke.

She made her way back to the master bedroom to find her phone. She picked it up and dialed Sharp.

"Everything okay?"

"I'm fine. Brittany was just here, though. She confirmed what I saw. Mitch is at the barn and things are not looking good for him. Are the roads open yet?"

"I don't even care if they are. I'll find a way through." He disconnected.

Kahrren heard the line go dead and said to herself, "Okay, talk to you later. Bye now."

She flipped open her text message app and pulled up Lorna's name.

Kahrren: Thanks for breakfast. Where are you guys?

Lorna: Groceries. Beth and Katie are coming over this evening for girls' night. I accepted on your behalf.

Kahrren: Great! Haven't seen them in a while.

Lorna: Andrew is going to cook. Like a real meal.

Kahrren: Does that mean vegetables?

Lorna: Among other things, yes. Don't worry, there will be plenty of other stuff to eat.

Kahrren: Brittany came. Confirmed my last vision.

Lorna: Damn. Hoped she was wrong. Talk to you when we get home. At checkout!

She switched the text recipient to Sharp and sent: Please let me know if you make it out there. I am worried. And be careful!

She didn't hear back.

* * *

Sharp left Daniels at the station to work on phone calls and paperwork, with no explanation as to where he was going. Knowing full well he could get stuck, he made a stop at a market to get food and water, then headed east on I-84.

The local public radio station was broadcasting constant updates on the weather and road conditions. "At this time I-84 is closed in both directions between Troutdale and The Dalles. There are hundreds of cars waiting to get through as soon as the freeway opens, despite being told the clearing of the road may take through Sunday night. Efforts to restore the flow of traffic are being hampered by the continuous bombardment of roadways by what is being called a once in a lifetime storm event. Travelers are being rerouted despite their insistence on waiting."

"Just try and reroute me. See how it works out for you." Opting for one of the department's sports utility vehicles equipped with four-wheel drive, he'd planned to get through this mess come hell or high water, such as it may be.

Being a native to the Portland Metro area had its benefits. He knew how to navigate side streets better than almost anyone. He managed to avoid a large number of stationary cars by taking surface streets, until finally he had to get on the highway.

Despite using emergency lights and occasionally blaring his siren, he was moving at a glacial pace. The radio reiterated warnings not to attempt to traverse the Gorge. These admonitory messages were largely ignored, as evidenced by the mid-freeway parking lot in which he found himself. Trying to creep by on the shoulder past the impatient drivers who'd been stuck on the road for hours longer than he had been, was yielding limited results.

He came upon a bright red Porsche 911 Carrera stopped entirely on the left shoulder. The man in it had entirely abandoned his spot in the left lane and the cars remaining in the lane closed the space between them. No amount of honking or sirens had an impact on the driver. Sharp put his SUV in park and exited. He approached the car and knocked briskly on the driver's side window. The man jumped then cracked the window.

"Sir, you need to find a way to move your car immediately. I am a detective with the Portland PD. I have an emergency and have to get through." His badge shone proudly from his belt.

"Well, you can *see* I have nowhere to go." He gestured to the traffic defiantly, his tone slicing. "You're just going to have to wait like the rest of us."

"You've got two minutes to ask your neighbors here to make a space for your car before I plow right through it, *now get out of the car before I place you under arrest and have this piece of tin impounded.*" Sharp's dormant rage had risen quickly to the surface. He opened the man's car door and waited for him to exit the vehicle. "Now start knocking on these windows." Sharp took his badge from his belt and showed it to people in the surrounding cars, shouting *"Move these vehicles over, please! Let this guy back in!"* The driver followed Sharp's lead. Cars pulled forward and sideways to create space. It took the better part of half an hour, but eventually there was room for the luxury car to pull back in. Sharp looked at the man before he returned to his sports car. "You should be expecting a citation and an exceedingly large fine in the very near future. Now please, get in your car and stay in the damn lanes. If you go back onto the shoulder, you'll have one hell of a time keeping your driver's license. Now *move!*"

The Porsche driver moved his car back into the lane slowly, leaving Sharp ample time to take down his license plate information. "Dickhead," Sharp muttered as he drove by. He turned off the news station and radioed to units ahead explaining his impending arrival at the front. "Who's in charge up there?" he asked when he got through on the line.

"It's Sergeant Tarfor, sir."

"Copy." He set down the handset and continued on his way. He felt like he aged a decade in the amount of time it took him to get ahead of the traffic. He stopped the SUV in a vacant spot where it wouldn't be in the way. Tumbling out the door onto the roadway, a splash rose up and wet the bottom of his pant legs. "Shit."

He shut the door after grabbing his raincoat, putting it on as he walked across the road to find Sergeant Tarfor. Looking around, his heart sank. The road was a disaster. Reports that it was impassable were in no way exaggerated.

"Hello, Sergeant," he greeted the man as he approached a group of uniformed men standing in a huddle.

"Sharp! How the hell are ya?" Tarfor wiped the rain from his right hand on his pants before reaching to shake. "It's been a long time, my friend."

"Too long. It's good to see you. Listen, I know your hands are full with this mess, but I need to get through, no matter the cost. Can you help me?"

"What's going on?"

"My partner's in trouble. You know I'd never ask otherwise. I've already waited longer than I wanted to at the direction of my lieutenant, but I have to get over this so I can get up near Coopey Falls. And I need to do it yesterday."

"Sounds serious."

"Honestly, Ben, it's life or death."

Nodding his understanding, the sergeant keyed his radio and directed a boat be brought immediately back to the area. "It won't be easy. You're going to have to climb down the embankment and make your way to the boat. Someone will meet you there and take you around the obstruction. I'll have a vehicle meet you on the other side. Gibbs here will take you down to the water."

"You don't know how much I appreciate this. If you ever need anything…"

"Oh, don't you worry. I've got your number." He nodded to the officer waiting to guide him down to the river. "Now go. And be careful. It's a disaster down here but it won't be any better up in the woods."

Sharp patted him on the back and turned on his heel to meet Gibbs. After a short stop at his car to retrieve his provisions, his weapon, and his armor, he climbed, slipped, and fell his way down the embankment. By the time he was seated in the boat, he was muddy from head to toe.

"You okay, sir?" The young officer driving the boat made way immediately. "Sergeant Tarfor said you may need some help."

"I may indeed. How close can you get me to Coopey Falls?"

* * *

At the bottom of a second bottle of Malbec, Katie and Beth, the two friends Kahrren and Lorna had been closest to since college, decided some dancing was in order. Katie pulled Kahrren up by the arm. "Come on, Kahrren. You used to love to dance."

"That's because I used to be *able* to dance. Now all I can manage is swaying around my cane."

"That's good enough!" Katie danced around Kahrren as Beth sang at the top of her lungs to DNCE's "Cake by the Ocean."

"You know I don't like this music."

"Yup. Don't care. You can't dance to the depressing stuff you listen to." She took Kahrren by the wrist and swung her arm around gently, but in big sweeping motions.

"I'm gonna need my arm back, please. I'm losing my balance." Katie relinquished the arm and spun away.

Beth shouted over the music, "Dinner is almost ready. Surely a preemptive calorie burn is in order!" She shimmied and bounced toward the kitchen and returned, dragging Lorna out with one hand and a new bottle in the other.

Lorna was a born dancer and broke free of Beth's grasp, whirling around the living room. Beth's tall, willowy frame joyously spun away in her own direction.

"Woohoo!" Lorna erupted, and began singing along with the chorus of the song. She shimmied over to Kahrren, her off key warbling so loud it would likely crack a decibel meter clean in half. "Are you having fun?" she shouted.

"I need to sit." She stepped back and lowered herself to the couch, pulling her legs up onto the cushions.

As they waited for Andrew to ring the dinner bell, Beth opened the third bottle of wine and refilled the glasses on the table. "Kahrren, why aren't you drinking?"

"I should probably take it easy with my medication." The lie tasted bitter as it spilled from her mouth. The truth was she was too exhausted by her recovery, her work with the police, and her worry about Mitch to be interested in cutting loose like the rest of her friends.

Beth's head leaned toward her shoulder as she gazed at Kahrren. She sat next to her friend. "Are you okay?"

"Tired. Achy. I'm not used to entertaining much these days."

"Can you really not drink?"

Red crept up Kahrren's neck and into her face. "Don't be mad."

"Here," she said and handed Kahrren her glass. "I'm not mad. But maybe a little bit will help."

"Thanks." She sipped and moaned her approval. "That's nice." Smiling at Beth, she reached out and squeezed her forearm gently.

A very handsome, green-eyed man with curly, dark hair stepped from the kitchen wearing an apron over slacks and a black sweater. "Ladies, your dinner is ready. Will you be eating out here or will you come to the table?"

"Table, please. I don't wanna be cleaning up after this drunken coven." Kahrren rose from the couch. "Now all of you go while I change the music. I can't take another minute of this."

"You better put on something fun!" Lorna wagged her finger as she crossed the living room behind Katie and Beth, stopping momentarily to smooch her boyfriend. "Thanks for dinner. It smells amazing."

"You're welcome. I'm glad you're having fun." He pressed another kiss to her lips before she disappeared. "Kahrren?" Andrew approached her as she stood facing the entertainment center.

"Yes?"

"Thank you for turning that music off." His grimacing face quickly disappeared into the kitchen.

Kahrren grinned from ear to ear as she put on the upbeat music requested and made her way to the dining nook in the kitchen. "Everybody here loves eighties music so I put on an upbeat playlist. Do not complain or I will change my selection." She held her cell phone out showing them a pre-selected alternative option of The Cure's *Disintegration* album. "I have depressing music and I'm not afraid to use it."

"Sit. No one is going to argue with the eighties." Lorna started dishing a plate for Kahrren, one for Andrew, and one for herself. Katie and Beth followed her lead, each starting on their own.

Andrew came to the table with a serving dish filled with something Lorna had requested, but he'd never previously made.

"What are these? They smell great." Katie stuck her as yet unused fork into the pile of what appeared to be meatballs.

"Lorna asked for buffalo chicken meatballs. So chicken, bleu cheese, and buffalo sauce, breaded and deep fried. This bottle is blue cheese dressing, and the other one is ranch." He set the dish on a trivet next to the dressing.

Beth craned her neck forward trying to catch a glimpse of this addition to the table. "Will you marry us?" she joked.

Andrew flashed his legendary lady-killing smile. "I should be so lucky." He turned once more to grab two more bowls. "Green salad and marinated veggies." Catching Kahrren's sneer, he added, "You had it before and said you liked it. I believe you used the word 'un-vegetable-y'."

"Oh! *That* stuff? I'll eat that." She took a heaping scoop of sliced tomato, cucumber, artichoke hearts, pepperoncini and green olives which had been bathing in a sweet red wine vinaigrette for hours. "Un-vegetable-y indeed."

Lorna beamed at Andrew as Katie and Beth exchanged exaggerated looks of bewilderment. "You can all shut up," Kahrren defended, to a chorus of chortles. "I do *occasionally* eat vegetables."

What was supposed to be several days' worth of food was obliterated by the assemblage of persons leaving the kitchen after Andrew's refusal to allow them to assist in cleaning up. Light chatter floated through the air to his ear as the kitchen returned to a semblance of order which it normally exhibited.

Planning to slip past the living room and into the bedroom to allow girls' night to continue, his plan was foiled, only steps from his intended destination.

"*Lorna!*" Kahrren's voice was sharp and acidic. "*What the hell are you doing?*" Andrew backpedaled to the living room.

Lorna's hand raised and pressed against her lips. "Oh, my God. I'm *so sorry,* Kahrren. I didn't mean to." Her eyes searched Kahrren's face.

Beth's head was shaking back and forth, her silence said more than any gesture could.

Katie tried reasoning. "No. She's just intuitive. There's no such thing as psychics."

Lorna wrapped her arms around her knees and pulled them into her chest. "I really didn't mean to, Kahrren."

"And so am I supposed to feel better?" Her voice was pure acid. "I'm going to bed."

Beth threw her hands up in front of Kahrren. "Like hell you are. We aren't done here. Not by a longshot."

"Damn it, Lorna. *You* should have to be the one to explain all of this and do the inevitable round of parlor tricks to prove you're not a liar." Trying her damndest to suppress the sob fighting to escape, she punched one of Lorna's stupid throw pillows. *"Fine.* What do you want to know?" She looked at Beth, then at Katie. "It's true. I'm psychic." She threw herself backward on the couch and growled, "I hate that *fucking* word."

Andrew slipped in and sat next to Lorna, wrapping his arm around her shoulder. She leaned into him.

"How does it work?" Katie asked.

"And why didn't you tell us before?" Beth's foot shook furiously, as her voice grew loud and demanding.

"I don't like talking about it, that's why." Kahrren barked the comment at Beth.

"Hey, you're out of line. I'm not the one hiding things from my friends. Keep shouting at me and see what happens next." Beth's tone was all challenge. She may as well have slapped Kahrren with a white glove.

"This isn't *fucking* about you, Beth. Maybe I shouldn't have been snippy with you. You didn't create this situation. But, you know what? *Neither did I.* I didn't choose to be like this." Kahrren sat forward placing one arm on her knee and pointing at Beth with the index finger of her other hand. "You wanna know why I don't tell people about it? Because I don't want to deal with shit like this. Why don't you try being a little more understanding about how this affects *me*? It has nothing to do with you! I don't owe you an explanation about this. Or anything else, for that matter." She sat back and crossed her arms protectively. "Looks like I was right. I can't trust any of you with this."

Lorna jumped up onto her knees and pointed her finger at Kahrren. "Now wait a minute! That's not fair! I—"

"*Calm* down, tiny tot. You have to agree, this would be easier if I hadn't told anyone." Kahrren squeezed her eyes tightly, then heaved a deep sigh and opened them. Her face was red and her head was starting to pound. She rubbed her temples for a few seconds, before continuing. "Look, I don't want to fight. This thing is what it is. Believe me or don't. I am sick of becoming a trick pony every time someone finds out about what I can do." She grabbed the bottle of pain pills that sat on the table next to her normal spot on the couch. She took two pills as indicated on the label.

Beth pressed her fingers to her lips, her normally rigid posture collapsing into a sag. "Jesus, Kahrren. Are you all right?" Beth's tone had changed dramatically. "I'm sorry. I didn't realize you were dealing with this at all, much less that it was such a big deal."

"Just forget it. Now everyone knows. There's nothing I can do. My head is pounding and I need to go to bed, so let's get this over with." Kahrren continued, trying desperately to keep her temper in check. "I have had this ability my whole life. It used to be only when I touched things. Since that psycho almost beat me to death and damaged my brain back in the spring, it's kind of been in overdrive. I see and hear things all the time without having to touch anything."

Andrew looked at Kahrren pointedly. She clicked her tongue and rolled her eyes. "And sometimes I see dead people."

Chapter Nine

D etective Daniels tossed his cell phone on the desk after the fourth failed attempt to reach Sharp. He rose and crossed the office to Rodriguez's office. "Still not picking up, sir."

"Fine. I'll continue trying to reach him. Find someone who isn't busy and take them with you to make the arrest. The warrant is in your inbox. Get a move on. You don't want the guy to disappear on you."

Daniels nodded, then returned to his desk. He pocketed his cell, slid on his suit coat, and topped it with his raincoat. He grabbed the warrant from his inbox and came across the brand new detective assigned to the squad. "Are you doing anything important?"

"No, sir. Busy work until Rodriguez lets me know otherwise."

"Get your coat. What's your name?"

"Wynn Garrett, sir."

"I'm Daniels. Don't call me sir." He grabbed the coat from the back of Garrett's chair and lightly tossed it to him. "Where did you come from?"

"Vice. But I got tired of hookers and blow, so thought I'd kick it up a notch."

Daniels marched the short distance to Rodriguez's office. "I'm taking Garrett. He doesn't have anything better to do."

"Perfect. Let me know how he does."

Daniels nodded and returned to the fresh, young detective. "So, how'd you end up with a name like that?" There was a twinkle in his eye as he smiled.

"Just lucky, I guess." His short blonde hair and blue-grey eyes gave him an all-American look, but his cheeky comments and tone of voice hinted at something a little more fun.

"Have you ever arrested a murderer, Garrett?"

"No. But I shot one though."

"Well, well. Aren't you full of surprises?"

* * *

Kahrren made her way to the living room to find she was the first one up. Katie was cuddled up beneath a blanket on the couch. Beth lay sprawled across an air mattress. The room was dark owing to the blackout curtains Lorna had over every window of the townhouse.

The kitchen was once again untidy after the previous evening's gathering. *How can four tiny women and one average man consume so much junk? And didn't Andrew clean up after dinner?* Not only had they eaten all of the food Andrew prepared, but also gone were a bag of chips, several bottles of wine, at least one whole block of cheese, a box of crackers, the whole stash of candy and two gallons of ice cream. The thought nauseated her.

She pulled the carafe from the coffee maker and after filling it transferred the water to the machine. Once the lid was off the coffee can, she raised it to her nose and breathed in the aroma, then began scooping grounds into a paper filter. The coffee set to brew, Kahrren started sorting through the mess left on the counter from after dinner snacking and drinks. She placed garbage into the bin, bottles into the recycling bag, and dishes into the dishwasher. She wiped the counters and washed her hands.

Holding a cup of coffee, she quietly returned to her bedroom and set it on the nightstand. Situated on the bed, she grabbed the remote and flipped on the tv. She swore under her breath once she settled on the news. She watched for a while before reaching for her phone.

The phone rang a few times before, unexpectedly, Sharp picked up. "You got something for me?"

"Nothing new. Sorry. I wanted to check in with you since I hadn't heard back." She paused, listening. "Where are you?"

"I'm in the gorge at the bottom of a hill I need to be on top of. I got dropped off by one of the local guys out here but no one is allowed up the hill right now because they're afraid it's going to slide."

"How far back is the barn? Could you come at it from a different direction?"

Sharp was quiet for a few very pronounced seconds. "Well, I guess we're about to find out." Staying true to form he hung up without indication he was going to do so.

Kahrren set down her phone, shaking her head. "I don't think I'll ever get used to that." She looked up as her door opened. "Morning," she said to Lorna, who crawled up on the bed next to her.

"Morning. How long have you been up?"

"Almost an hour. Made coffee. Cleaned up the post-dinner snacking mess in the kitchen."

"How did you accomplish so much?"

"Well, I didn't drink half the wine in Portland last night."

"Oh." Lorna smirked up at Kahrren, half her face buried in the pillow. She turned toward the tv. "Any progress out there?"

"No. And I just talked to Sharp. He hasn't made it up to the barn yet. They won't let him up the mountain because they are worried about mudslides. I suggested an alternate route so he is looking into it."

"This whole thing is so scary. I hope they find Mitch and he is okay."

"Me, too." Kahrren stopped herself from saying, *But...*

The door pushed even further open when Andrew came in with two cups of coffee. He set one down for Lorna on the nightstand, and seeing Kahrren had one already, he sat on the edge of the bed and kept the second mug for himself. He sipped and said, "How in hell are you up before everyone else?"

"You guys all went nuts last night. I didn't even finish one glass of wine."

"Oh." His response being so similar to Lorna's made Kahrren giggle. "Did you clean?"

"Mmhmm. And made the coffee you're enjoying."

"Our little girl is all grown up, darling." Lorna giggled. "Pretty soon she'll be moving out on her own."

"Ha!" Kahrren exclaimed. "It's coming sooner than you think. Like it or not."

Lorna blinked rapidly at the comment. "What do you mean?"

"Lorna, I'm getting better. As much as I love staying with you, I am ready to have my own place again, and I am *sure* you two would like some time alone. New relationships are important. You don't need me as a third wheel forever."

Andrew's face stayed perfectly blank as he sipped his coffee. Lorna sat up and faced Kahrren. "If I have my way, you'll be here forever. And I told him so."

"Andrew? What do you have to say about this?"

"Oh, no. This is between the two of *you*. We have discussed it and I have been well informed that Lorna plans to have you here as long as she can manage it."

"I already know what Lorna thinks. But you're on Team Kahrren, aren't you, buddy?" Kahrren grinned at him and his face cracked into a smile.

"Hashtag team Kahrren," he agreed.

"*Hashtag team Kahrren stays with Lorna!*" Lorna's voice rose an octave and became shrill.

"Calm yourself, Lorna. You're not a toddler. Screaming won't get you your way." Kahrren's eyes were full of mischief. "I'm not leaving yet, but I am leaving at some point. It's always been the plan."

"I hate the plan," Lorna said glumly.

"It's a good plan, babe," Andrew added to Lorna. "At least she is here for now. We'll sort out the rest later. Now, let's go make breakfast for our guests."

* * *

With the majority of police officers out in the city assisting with the disastrous storm conditions, Rodriguez had little time for training his new detective. Exacerbating the situation, when he'd reached Sharp, he learned that his best detective was out on a wild goose chase, trying to find his missing partner.

He said to Daniels, "Since you're back, for now I need you and Garrett helping with 9-1-1 calls and taking reports. Once we get through this mess, we'll get him some proper training. If any homicide cases come in, I'll pull you off and send you out with Garrett again."

"Yes, sir. I'll let him know." Making his way to the young, new detective, he beckoned him with a quick sideways head jerk. "We're on calls until there's a homicide case."

"Well, aren't we the lucky ones?"

A couple of hours passed before Daniels darted into Rodriguez's office. "Sir, I think you may want to look at this."

"Tell me," he said, eyes focused on his computer screen.

"It's a report of burglary on a commercial property."

"So?" His fatigue was evident in his curt tone.

"So, this property owner said it's on the outskirts of town and someone had been in there."

"Get to the damn point, Daniels."

"The building has been abandoned for a couple of years but still has equipment inside. It used to be a meat packing plant. Drains in the floors and the whole shabang. This guy said there was a bunch of stuff he didn't leave in there."

Rodriguez held his hand out for the report and squinted at it. "Get down there and see if this could be where the victim was killed and placed in the cube. Take Garrett, and I'll get some folks on standby to process the scene if you tell me you think it's related."

"Yes, sir. I'm on it." Daniels collected Garrett and the pair headed to the car. "You did a good job arresting that guy earlier. Let's see how you do interviewing this one." He handed Garrett the file to review on the drive over and briefed him on what was known about the case.

They trudged through the pouring rain to a man waiting outside a rusty door. The building was on an old, isolated lot with grass growing up through the cracked pavement in the parking lot. The building owner held the door open for them and followed them in.

Though the warehouse was lit, it was dim and dingy inside. "Thanks for coming," the man said. "I'm Edwin Willis. I own the property. Please come this way."

The detectives followed Mr. Willis to a table in the middle of the room. Next to the table there was a drain in the floor, multiple bottles of chemicals, boxes, and old, bloody tools. "None of this was here when I checked the place out last month. The table wasn't here, and none of these boxes or bottles were here."

"What made you come here today, with weather like this?" Garrett asked the man.

"I had it on my schedule to do today so I can show it to an interested buyer next week." He lifted his hands, palms up. "I don't live too far away and the streets were passable so I came."

Garrett nodded. "The buckets and tools, were they here?"

"The tools might have been. There are a bunch of leftover tools from the meat-packing business, but I can't say for sure." He pointed to the remaining detritus. "That stuff I've never seen. I didn't touch it, but I did lean down and look at one of the shipping labels. It's got a date from a couple of weeks ago, and I know they never used resin when it was a meat place."

"Mr. Willis, is it okay with you if we have some investigators come in to collect evidence?"

"Absolutely. I'll put off the potential buyers, and you all can do whatever you need to do." He shook his head. "There's a lockbox on the doorknob with a key in it. There's no alarm." He pulled a business card and pen from his jacket pocket. "Here is the lockbox combination."

"Thank you for your cooperation, Mr. Willis. Is the number on this card the best way to reach you?"

"It is."

"We'll be in touch."

* * *

"Kahrren?" the soft, normally bubbly voice seemed disturbed.

"Brittany? Are you okay?"

"Does the name Enoch Keres mean anything to you?"

Kahrren's eyes widened and her mouth fell open. "Enoch Keres has him?"

Brittany nodded, solemnly. "It's him. And it's bad. Sharp needs to get there *now.*"

"Do you know where it is, Brittany? Could you give me directions?"

Brittany nodded, then said, "Umm... like... I don't know the streets or anything."

"Tell me how to get there."

* * *

The phone picked up after the first ring. "Bub, it's me."

"What's wrong, Miss?"

"Can they fly a helicopter in this?"

"I beg your pardon?"

"If we don't get to Detective Adams right away, he isn't going to make it."

"Miss, this weather is bad. We may not have visibility. And where exactly do you think we'd be taking this helicopter?"

"To the same barn he was held at as a kid. Weren't you there?"

"Yes, I was. With your daddy. You know that. How do you know this?"

Her voice lowered. "You know how I know this, Bub."

There was a torturous moment of silence. "I'll have them get it ready."

"I'm coming with you."

"Like hell." A booming knock sounded on his front door. He opened the door and groaned.

"Just try and stop me."

Chapter Ten

"Sir, this way." Though the burly young man was outfitted head to toe for wet weather, he was so muscular, you could see his heft despite the bulk of his gear. "The truck is waiting to take us to the ATV. It's a side by side so we'll both fit. Sergeant Tarfor notified us you were coming, and you needed to get through some mud, so I'm your man, sir. No one knows this terrain like I do, so I'll drive, and you hang on for dear life."

"What's your name?" Sharp had never been so relieved to see a smoke eater in his life.

"I'm Carter, sir." He nodded his head decisively over his shoulder indicating they should go. "Am I correct in understanding time is of the essence?"

"Jim Sharp. Thank you for your help today." Sharp started the direction of the truck. "And yes, you are correct. You know where the barn is a couple miles back from Coopey Falls?"

Carter flashed a dazzling white smile through the muddy, wet facade. "I sure do. Used to go up there a lot a few years back." He opened the truck door for Sharp. "I haven't been up there in conditions like this, but I'll get you up there no problem. Are you looking for a quiet approach?" The truck blazed down the road as Carter gathered information.

"That's probably wise. I don't know what we'll find when we get there, but chances are, it's not gonna be good." Sharp pulled out his phone. "Excuse me a moment, Carter. I need to report what I'm up to." He dialed Rodriguez and waited for the line to connect. It took a moment but the line picked up eventually. "I'm going up to the barn after Adams. I got a guy who's good with muddy conditions. He's gonna try to get me up there. Any other info you have for me?"

Carter could hear Rodriguez shouting as Sharp held the phone away from his ear. "Yeah, we have SWAT preparing to deploy as well. The chief is trying to get a team up there with a bird. I'll make them aware you are heading up there as well. How are you getting there?"

"ATV until we are as close as we can get without being heard, then on foot."

"Copy. I can't get up there so let me know as soon as you have an update."

"Will do." Sharp disconnected, and shook his head, pocketing his phone. He could feel his heart pounding and the crushing weight of anxiety gripping his chest. He looked at Carter and the driver, who was a lovely, if windswept, redhead in her thirties with the name Doyle embroidered on her coat. "Anybody else ready for this day to be over?"

Doyle answered, "Very much so, but today is going to last for probably three more days, if I had to guess." She grinned a good-natured but tired smile. "I was just coming off a forty-eight when I got called back."

"Ouch," Sharp commiserated.

"Not me, sir. I live for this shit."

"How old are you, Carter? And you don't have to call me sir. Jim is fine. Or Sharp."

"Okay, Jim. I'm twenty three."

"I can't even remember twenty three."

"But I bet you've seen some really amazing stuff. Things I won't get to see for a very long time, if ever." Carter's enthusiasm would have been infectious under other circumstances.

"I have seen some pretty intense stuff, that's for sure. Most of it was the stuff of nightmares." Sharp paused. "For today, I only hope we can get to my partner before it gets any worse for him."

"What are we facing?"

"Hostage situation with extreme violence and the possibility he's already dead. The *sick fuck* we believe is holding him hostage is likely armed. I want you to stay back where he can't see you."

Sharp watched Carter's face twist as he tried to control himself. "If you insist."

"I do. The last thing I need is another exceptional young man ending up as a casualty at the feet of this son of a bitch. Also, you heard my lieutenant, They're trying to get SWAT up there. We don't need to be in their way. Either one of us."

"Copy that." The remaining few minutes in the truck were spent in silence as the men mentally prepared for their endeavor.

The frigid air blasted them in the face as they disembarked from the truck. As Sharp stowed his bag containing a bulletproof vest and extra ammunition on the back of the vehicle, Carter raced around the ATV, performing a rapid series of checks for safety. Tire pressure, engine check, fuel, and emergency provisions all checked out. "Welcome aboard. Please strap in and hang on. If we roll, do your very best to keep your arms inside. Unless you like having them crushed, then, by all means… flail away."

"Thanks for the tip. Let's get moving."

"You've come to the right place." Carter jumped in and secured his safety belt, then fired up the engine. The loud roar vibrated Sharp's ears with pulsating pressure as it carried the grizzled old detective and the eager young firefighter into the woods in search of the missing detective.

"Where'd you learn how to drive like this, Carter?"

"I grew up back here. I've been doing this all my life."

"How'd you get to be in Fire and Rescue?"

"Forestry was a little slow for me, so I changed it up. But I still know some guys. They called me to come help." He grinned, "Normally my gig is to put the wet stuff on the hot stuff, ya know? Gotta start somewhere. But I am working toward being a paramedic too."

"Good luck, kid. They're lucky to have you."

Carter nodded. "Thank you. Grab onto the oh shit bar, sir!"

Sharp got his hand around the safety bar as the passenger side of the utility vehicle went up and over a boulder that would have come to Sharp's knees if he were standing. Carter's grin somehow seemed wider than his actual face. Sharp was enjoying the journey significantly less, gripping the metal handle with both hands in an effort not to let his weight topple onto the young firefighter. "If it's *at all* possible to avoid the maneuver you just did in the future, it would be most appreciated."

"I'll see what I can do, sir."

The bumps, jostles, and splashes the two faced were more than Sharp had bargained for. He wasn't so good with motion like this. Pulling his head back in after retching, he asked, "How long until we get there?"

"Maybe an hour. It's going to get a bit tricky up ahead, then we should sail right through."

"Tricki-*er?*"

"Afraid so."

"Perfect." Were it not covered in mud, his face would have been green, which was very different from Carter, who seemed to be enjoying every moment. "You gonna be able to do this in the dark?"

"Hell, that's when it's the most fun!" Carter cackled like he had just escaped an asylum in a superhero film.

"God help me."

* * *

The gray skies over the Columbia River Gorge offered little light even at the peak of the day. With sunset impending, the light was failing quickly. Light wind blew Kahrren's hair over her face as she leaned in to hear the conversation taking place before her.

"Sir, this is against protocol. She should *not* be here." Though his words were firm, Sergeant Carruthers's tone was respectful while addressing Chief Donovan. As the overall team leader, he was responsible for everything that happened during a mission. "She's a civilian, sir. I can't let her on this bird."

"You can do exactly what I tell you to do, or you can hand in your badge.

She is a consultant, and she *will* be accompanying me." Donovan's rock solid scowl was as dominating as his presence. Sergeant Carruthers mashed his lips together and inhaled, closing his eyes, and nodding a reluctant assent, his face burning a fiery red. "Good. Now find a place for us on this helicopter."

"With me then, Chief, miss." He waved them toward the waiting Blackhawk helicopter and directed them into seats which would be out of the way for the disembarkation. He handed a headset first to Kahrren, then to the chief. Once Kahrren's ears were covered with the device, Carruthers looked at her and asked, "Can you hear me?"

"Loud and clear," she responded.

"Good. I'll help you get buckled. Don't take your headset off unless we tell you, all right?" His eyes met hers and he waited for her to agree. His fingers danced deftly over her abdomen, buckling her snugly into place. He looked over his shoulder at the Chief who was neither taking his seat, nor did he have his headset in place. "So, what kind of consultant are you?"

Her lips pulled back in a contrived smile. *Time for the freak show.* "A psychic one." She watched his face, and answering his real questions, she said, "No, I'm not his girlfriend. No, this is not a joyride. Yes, I am a real consultant." His jaw went slack as her smile became cavalier. "I'm the one who found him the last time, and I am the one who found him again."

Carruthers pulled his head back and he questioned, "This guy has been rescued before?"

"Yes, but he was only about eight at the time."

"How old is he now? I thought he was a cop. Wait, how old are *you?*"

A booming voice interrupted as Kahrren tried to answer. "He *is* a cop. A homicide detective. We believe he is in danger, or you wouldn't be here." Donovan always sounded intimidating but this evening, he was downright ferocious. "Don't you have something better to do than flirt with her?"

"We weren't flirting!" Kahrren and Carruthers blurted in unison.

Carruthers moved back and situated himself in his seat, taking the time to calm himself. Once accomplished, he began his rundown of the operation. Kahrren watched the group of men, each of whom had unshakeable focus. A torrent of technical police jargon flew by as she sat quietly, waiting. She looked at Bub who sat quietly listening and nodding his head in approval. Though he appeared calm, she picked up on the heavy feeling in his chest. *He's afraid.* She gently placed her tiny hand over his massive paw and squeezed.

He looked at her. He didn't smile. There was no change in his expression. He just gazed at her. She heard him thinking. *You better be right about this.*

She mouthed, "I am."

Bub's eyes bugged out for the briefest of moments before he smoothed his face. He exhaled and reciprocated her squeeze, then pulled his hand back. *Touching her is weird now,* she heard him think. Placing her hand back in her own lap, she found a spot on the floor and stared at it.

She never expected Bub to know about her ability. Now that he did, things were going to get awkward. And it really hurt. She closed her glassy eyes, trying her damndest not to full-on ugly cry.

With her lack of focus she started picking up on the undercurrent of thoughts which had begun pouring from the men as they sat quietly waiting for departure. Carruthers and the other team leaders had finished their review, so they were moments from taking off. Not surprisingly, most of these men started out thinking about the operation, but soon switched to thoughts of their families. Images of smiling kids and loving wives flashed over and again in Kahrren's mind. Every man on this flight had something beautiful to come home to. She hoped they would all make it back.

The blades were spinning, and the engine was warming. It was almost time. The increase in energy was palpable as the helicopter lifted off.

* * *

Every part of Mitch's body throbbed. His head had been aching since it was smashed with a rock a couple of days earlier. His back, shoulders and hips agonized from being splayed for so long. The abuse he had endured since then had done a number on every part of his body. The rope binding his wrists and ankles, securing him to the bed was so tight, all he could feel of his hands and feet was the sharp pain that came with lack of circulation.

"Stop whimpering. We're almost done." Enoch Keres was painted head to toe with mud. "As soon as I can get the hole deep enough, it'll be over. Not too long now."

Mitch didn't realize he had been vocalizing. Slipping intermittently into unconsciousness from traumatic exhaustion and god knows what was in his water, he woke repeatedly, weeping. His voice quavered, "Why are you doing this?"

"Now, I thought you would remember from the last time…" Keres leaned in, tickling Mitch's ear with his lips, "that we didn't quite get to finish." He rose, moved to the window, and pulled back the shaggy blanket which was serving as a curtain. The plastic sheeting he'd used to black out the windows had long since rotted away. "And I never leave anything unfinished."

"Please… please let me go. You'll never see me again. I won't try to find you."

Keres chuckled. "Oh, I know you won't. I won't give you the opportunity." The sound of his footsteps moved from one window to the other. "And I plan on being long gone by the time anyone figures out where you are. Then I can get back to business."

"What business?"

"Oh, haven't you figured it out yet? I learned about a new hobby in prison. There was lots of time to read, so I read anything I could get my hands on. I know about woodworking, gardening, making furniture, computer networking, bird watching… Hell, I even got a college degree when I was locked up, in Human anatomy and pathology. I also picked up an interest in arts and crafts." He snickered as he moved toward Mitch and stood over him. "I've really been into *resin* lately."

"Oh, we knew it was you."

"That so? How'd you figure it out?"

"He had the same injuries as I had when I was a kid." Mitch was holding onto consciousness with all his might. Focusing on work was how he always got through trauma. It was the only thing he could try. "And right after you were released from prison. It wasn't very smart if you ask me. They call it a pattern of conduct. Anyone found with similar injuries is gonna get pinned on you now."

"That's only if they catch me, which'll be really hard if I'm not around."

"And just where do you think you'll be?"

"Oh, far away. That's all you need to know."

"I may not make it out of here, but you picked a fight with the wrong cop. My partner is going to find me—dead or alive—and then he is going to find *you*."

"Mmhmm. We'll see." He pressed a water bottle to Mitch's lips. "Now drink. I'm tired of your yammering."

Mitch was so parched he drank as much as he could get in and welcomed the escape passing out provided.

Chapter Eleven

T he crime scene investigators spent hours at the warehouse, lifting every fingerprint, chemical bottle, blood drop and any other evidence that they could find which might possibly be related to the case.

Daniels and Garret stayed at the scene until there was no more use for them, then returned to the station to find Rodriguez sitting at his desk, leaning forward into his hand with his fingers through his thick, black hair. "News?" Rodriguez demanded as they walked into his office.

"The techs lifted anything and everything. Now we just have to wait for them to process it. There's a lot of evidence so we told them to prioritize anything related to the resin and fingerprints from the area surrounding where the bottles and boxes were found." Daniels stood, waiting for a response from Rodriguez.

"Fine. How'd Garrett do?"

Daniels looked over his shoulder to locate the young detective, who was well out of earshot. "He's doing great. Has a good head on his shoulders. I wouldn't mind if he stays with me as a partner. He's smart, asks the right questions, and knows when to stop talking. He's a natural."

"That's good. We'll keep him with you for a while. I'll presume he is still doing well unless I hear otherwise from you, so keep me updated."

"Yes, sir. Will do." Daniels turned to the door, then hesitated. "Is there any news about Adams or Sharp, sir?"

The lieutenant's face twisted in helpless frustration. "Sharp is on the way on an ATV. Chief Donovan is heading out with SWAT. No news of progress yet."

"Are the roads clearing up any?"

"Ha! Whatever progress they've made is going to be washed away with the next wave of storms which are supposed to come some time tonight. They are turning all the cars around on I-84, no longer allowing anyone to wait for the road to open. I don't even know how Sharp convinced them to let him through that mess."

Daniels grinned. "He can be very persuasive. And he knows everyone. I am sure he is calling in favors."

"Must be. He has better connections than I have, because I couldn't find anyone to get me through there. I've been on the phone since yesterday trying to find a way through, favors or not." He shook his head and shrugged one shoulder. "I've had no luck. But thankfully, people seem mostly to be staying in place. The board is clear for now, so go home and get some rest. Tell Garret to go too."

"Yes, sir. Please let me know if there is an update with Sharp and Adams. I like those guys."

"We all do." The men nodded to each other, and Daniels walked out.

"Go home and get some sleep, Garrett. LT's orders."

"God bless the man," the young detective said, his eyelids drooping.

* * *

Lorna: Where the hell did you go, Kahrren?

Lorna: Are you coming home for dinner?

Kahrren: Sorry, you were napping. I'm with Bub. Won't be home for dinner. Go have some quality time!

"She actually used the eggplant emoji. Can you *believe* that?" Lorna laughed boisterously after reading the text exchange aloud to Andrew.

"Well, it does sound rather nice, actually. Not only did she let you sleep, it looks like we have the house to ourselves for a while." He grinned devilishly. "Let's have our dinner, then we'll light some candles, have a bath, maybe some massage… and who knows what else."

"I know what else!" Lorna's grin was nothing short of wicked as she wiggled her eyebrows in an overexaggerated manner. "Hubba, hubba!" She settled herself into his lap and nuzzled her face into his neck. "You know, I am beginning to see the benefits of Kahrren returning to her own place," she cooed at him.

"I'll buy her one. Tomorrow," he joked. "I'm so on board." His soft laugh filled her senses with the promise of what solitude would bring.

"Let's skip dinner and go straight to the bath."

Needing no further encouragement, he lifted her up and carried her away for the evening.

The pair came up for air and food after a couple of hours and multiple… interludes. Standing in the kitchen in his robe, Andrew was munching away at some veggies and dip, waiting for some pasta to warm in the microwave. Lorna joined him and grabbed a carrot, dipped it in the dressing, and popped it in her mouth then scrunched her face.

"What's wrong?" Andrew asked.

"Ugh. I think I waited too long to eat. It happens sometimes. My stomach feels weird if I don't keep something in it. It's just a little nausea." She smiled up at him. "I'm fine. See?" She grabbed another piece of crudité and chomped on it. "How long until the pasta is done?"

"It should be almost ready. Go sit. I'll bring it to you."

"Thanks." She playfully swatted at his backside, then plopped down in a kitchen chair. "I'm starving."

"Me too. I don't think we eat as often when Kahrren isn't around. I mean… well, besides the obvious reason, she seems to always be hungry so there's always food when she's here. How is she so thin?"

"I don't know. Good genes? Before her attack she was also super active, whether she admits it or not. Massaging all day is really hard work. Plus she walked all the time. I think she secretly ran on a treadmill or rode a bike or something because she has always been a big eater."

Andrew set the plate in front of her. "Here you go." He sat across from her. "You hold your own with her though. I have seen how you eat."

"Yep. I do love to eat. But what you haven't seen is yoga three times a week with Katie, walking or running every day, going dancing every week, and cardio workouts before work every day. *I* have to work for it, Beth is another one who can eat anything and everything with no effect on her body. It's not fair. Katie eats a lot but exercises for a living. We have to work for it but Beth and Kahrren have tapeworms or something." Lorna took a big bite of creamy pasta. After she swallowed she said, "Mmm, worth every step."

Their late dinner finished, the two returned to their bedroom for some sleep. Lorna made sure her ringer was on in case anyone needed her, then fell first into Andrew's embrace, then Morpheus's.

* * *

A break in the rain served as a small blessing on the approach to the cabin, though the sky was still hidden behind a thick, low-hanging layer of clouds. Carter was looking a little unsettled by the jostling the pair endured over the last half a mile or so, and Sharp had practically heaved himself inside out with sickness.

Carter slowed and shut down the engine and lights. "I think this is about as close as we can get knowing for sure the vehicle won't be heard." He unbuckled and jumped out of the driver's seat. Unzipping a heavy duffel bag, he grabbed a couple flashlights. "I know you want me to stay far away, and I will, but you still need me to get you there. Besides the fact that you don't know where you're going, it's not safe to be out there on your own."

Sharp extracted himself from the passenger seat and stood next to Carter behind the ATV. He took his bag from Carter's hands as soon as the young man removed it from the pile of mud-soaked supplies. Once the bag was unzipped, he pulled out his armor, slid it over his torso, and secured it. Once he'd placed all the extra ammunition he could carry on various parts of his body, he took the flashlight the young man handed him, peering back from the corners of his eyes. "You'll back away when I tell you?"

"I absolutely will. There's a reason I didn't join the police, my friend. I have no desire to get shot."

"Neither do I. Let's do this. Anything I need to know?"

"Yeah. If the land starts sliding, don't try to outrun it, move sideways instead. Don't hide behind trees, they'll take you out fast. If you fall and get caught in it, curl up and protect your head. Uh… water flow deviating from normal is a bad sign. Point out to me if you see it either speed up or slow down from what's around it." Carter slung a backpack around his torso and clipped the straps in place. "You already know this is dangerous. Ask me if you are unsure of something. Follow my footsteps as closely as you can. Pay attention to noises that seem out of place and let me know if you think you hear something."

"Easy enough."

"Good. Let's do this." Taking the lead, the young firefighter walked ahead.

As nearly as Sharp could tell, they came from southeast of where the cabin sat, but were now hiking in a southwestern direction. "Did we pass it?"

"Yeah, a little bit. It was the best way around. I had to go a bit north, which is why we're heading south-southwest now."

Sharp grunted his understanding. "You know, I think I'll take a vacation after this."

"Yeah? Where are you gonna go?"

"Somewhere warm and dry, for damn sure."

"No one could blame you for that. Ever been to the desert? There are some really amazing places in the southwest."

"Not yet. Maybe I'll give it a shot."

"I hope you do. Seems like this must be really hard. I sure hope everything turns out all right for your partner."

"Thanks, Carter. Me too." They walked on for a few more minutes, then Sharp asked, "Do you really do this for fun?"

Carter snickered. "Sure do. Turns out it's coming in handy. My grandma always used to say, 'You never know where a blessing's gonna come from.' Looks like she was right. I never imagined playing in the mud might save someone's life."

Sharp's thoughts turned to Kahrren. "Your grandma sure got that one right. They come from strange places, indeed." Sharp bumped into Carter, not realizing he had stopped abruptly. Seeing his flashlight was off and his hand waved in the air, Sharp hit the switch to his own light, and stood quietly. It took a moment for his eyes to adjust, but then he saw what Carter had spotted. A distant, dim light.

* * *

Kahrren jolted in the seat next to her godfather. She had been sitting peacefully—or as peacefully as possible—in a chopper filled with elite badasses, eyes closed, trying to keep herself together enough to get through the evening when she felt something tickle her nose. Her eyes opened and she blinked rapidly. Much to her chagrin she saw the grinning face of her least favorite bobble-headed apparition behind a swirling spectral finger circling in front of her face.

"Hiiiiiiieeeeee Kahrreeeeeeen! Look what I can do now!" Brittany reached out and touched Kahrren's arm. And damned if Kahrren didn't feel it. "You know, that Patrick Swayze movie had it all wrong. It doesn't work like that at all."

Not being in an appropriate situation to question Brittany's ghost out loud, Kahrren tilted her head and scowled, seemingly at thin air. She waited for more information from the pestering poltergeist, but when none was forthcoming, she rolled her eyes and looked away.

Realizing she had the upper hand, Brittany began what appeared to be a rather rousing game of "I'm not touching you, I'm not touching you, Oh, look! I'm touching you!" to which Kahrren was entirely helpless to respond without embarrassing herself, or worse, embarrassing Bub.

Shifting in her seat, she realized, after approximately the eight millionth round of Brittany's game—each one followed by an evil, spectral cackle, Kahrren rapidly flung her left leg up and out in the air in front of her, then crossed it over her right leg, which was still planted on the floor.

When Bub gave her a questioning look and asked, "Are you all right?" she smiled back at him.

"My knee gives me some trouble since… It's fine."

"I can't believe you freaking kicked me!" Being dead didn't stop Brittany from being indignant.

Kahrren lowered her eyes to her hands which were folded neatly on her lap and smiled.

"See if I help *you* again!" Brittany turned in a slow circle, gawking at each of the men in turn. "Ooh, I'd help him, though. *Nice.*" She drew the word out in a long display of appreciation.

Kahrren mashed her lips together and tucked them in far enough between her teeth to bite down on them. It was the only thing she could do to control her smile. *What a paranormal pain in the ass,* she thought.

As if in response, Brittany whipped around and looked directly into Kahrren's eyes. Her lips didn't move, but Kahrren heard her, regardless. *God, are you always this rude?*

Wait. Can you hear me, Brittany?

Brittany sauntered back toward the front of the cabin, where Kahreen was seated. "Know what I've always wanted to try, Kahrren?"

Kahrren lifted her face in inquiry.

"Skydiving." Brittany threw herself straight through the fuselage and disappeared.

"You total cow."

Every head on board turned her direction.

"Uh… sorry. I was just thinking out loud."

* * *

The short respite from the storm ended abruptly with a booming roll of thunder. Violent rain dumped over every tree, car, and building in and around Portland. The evacuation of the roadways was still underway, but not yet near completion.

Lieutenant Marco Rodriguez stood in the break room, drinking what was approximately his eighth cup of coffee of the day. The station was nearly empty since most uniformed officers were out on assignment and non-essential personnel had been sent home due to inclement conditions. The time was 8:32 PM.

A bespectacled young woman Rodriguez had seen around the station, but with whom he had never interacted, walked toward his office. She moved so quickly, he barely caught a glimpse of her as she walked by. He stepped out of the small room containing the world's worst coffee and a refrigerator full of expired food. "I'm the only one here. Who are you looking for?" His face was drawn but his tone was friendly.

"Lieutenant Rodriguez. Do you know him?" Her blue-gray eyes peered at him from behind purple frames. She was modestly dressed in a cream-colored boat-necked blouse which was carefully paired with a matching gray, black and cream plaid pencil skirt.

"I'm Rodriguez. What can I do for you?"

"I was asked to put these fingerprint results directly into your hands. Looks like you have a match for a recently released criminal." She peered down at the document, her chocolatey hair falling forward over her shoulders. "Enoch Keres. Does that sound familiar?"

"These are the prints collected from the meat packing plant today?" He took the proffered paper and looked at it.

"Yes, sir. One of the detectives at the scene today, Daniels, insisted this come directly to you. He asked me to run this first. I hope you found what you need."

He shook his head in disbelief. "We sure did." Newly invigorated by the results in his hand, the fact the psychic was actually right, and knowing everyone was on the right track to find Adams put a pep in his step that eight cups of coffee couldn't. Moving quickly toward his office he shouted back, "Thank you, Miss—Sorry, what is your name?"

"Serena Hayes."

"Thank you, Miss Hayes. Excellent work."

Rodriguez hustled to the phone and dialed the chief directly. There was no answer. He texted Donovan, figuring he was likely unable to hear his phone over the noise of the helicopter.

Rodriguez: Identification from meat packing plant fingerprints confirmed as Enoch Keres. Submitting for arrest warrant.

* * *

Donovan's phone, though silenced, had vibrated in his hand. He lifted the device and swiped, revealing the text from Rodriguez. He nodded his head and banged out a response.

Kahrren saw his movements and looked in his direction. He lifted the phone for her to read the text messages.

You were right, Miss, he thought.

She looked at his face and projected a thought with all her might. *I know.*

If Bub could have jumped out of the seatbelt, or his skin, he looked like he would have. He leaned as far away from her as he could manage without unstrapping himself. *I need you to stop, Miss. I'm not ready.*

She nodded again, the corners of her mouth were pulling down as her body shrank down into her seat. She closed her flooding eyes.

The pilot announced their imminent arrival. The men began to shift around in preparation to unload as swiftly as possible. As the team prepared to rappel to the ground, Carruthers knelt in front of Kahrren and the chief. "We are going to open up the side hatch. You stay buckled in at least until this thing is on the ground." He looked at Kahrren. *"I think you should stay on this bird no matter what happens, but it's really up to him."* He turned to address Donovan. "Chief, what do you plan to do?"

"I'll stay aboard until we land, then I will make the determination on what happens next. Sergeant Carruthers, don't worry. We won't get in your way."

Carruthers nodded and returned to his team.

In a flurry of expert actions, all of a sudden, the side of the Blackhawk was open and black-clad men poured out, appearing to fall away. The ropes to which they were attached were invisible in the dark. After their lightning-fast egress, Kahrren and the chief were joggled as the machine lifted and tilted its way to a safe landing, less than two minutes away.

The pilot turned and found the chief. "Sir, you may disembark if you would like. We are about a ten minute walk from the target. We believe the sound of the storm obscured the sound of our approach, but I recommend staying back, just in case we're wrong." He nodded toward Kahrren, indicating *she* was the one who should be staying back.

"Kahrren, remove your harness. I will escort you off the helicopter *where you will stand next to me no matter what happens. Do you understand me?"*

"Yes, sir," she said. She unlatched the seatbelt and stood, then followed Bub toward the rear hatch. Accepting his arm to assist her, she made her way carefully down the ramp. Desperate to break the tension between them, she asked, "So, Bub? I'm a consultant?"

"Technically, yes."

"Excellent. To whom shall I send my invoice?" She grinned brazenly.

He laughed at her insolence. "Try Rodriguez. He is the one who brought you in on this."

"He is, indeed. I shall have my secretary prepare it and send it right over."

"You're gonna make Lorna do it?"

"I'm gonna make Lorna do it."

Chapter Twelve

E noch Keres stood in the corner of the room, shirtless with his pants unfastened. The earlier break in the rain had given him the opportunity to dig a hole sufficient to accommodate someone the size of Mitchell Adams.

He wiped the mud and sweat from his face with a wet towel before cleaning up his arms and torso. Serving time in prison had given him the opportunity not only to get an education, but to transform his body into a powerful, sinewy form. In his late fifties, he was stronger and more fit than most men regardless of their age.

Moving his eyes over the stillness of Mitch's prone body, Keres hooked the heel of one of his boots under the toe of the other, to remove it. He repeated the action on the other side and stepped backward to avoid soiling his socks any more than he had to. He'd scraped off as much of the muck as possible before entering the converted barn.

He licked his lips in anticipation of one last pleasure before making use of the hole he'd dug outside. Kneeling at Mitch's side, he placed a hand on the captive's shoulder and shook him. *It's no fun when he's unconscious.*

Keres stood and crossed the room to an old, rotting wooden table where his gun, keys, food, and water sat. He uncapped a bottle of water, double checking the seal was intact so he didn't mistakenly incapacitate himself.

Half the bottle was gone by the time Mitch started to stir. Keres leered at the man, feeling his desire stir. He finished his water in one fast glug and tossed the bottle aside. Eagerly, he began to pull his jeans down over his hips. He laid aside his garments and crossed the room.

There seemed to be little more Mitch could endure. He moaned, "I'd rather die. Just kill me." As skin pressed to skin, Mitch tried to writhe away from the contact of Keres's body. There was nowhere for him to go. He screamed as loudly as he could manage, the kind of scream that took every ounce of fight he had left in him.

* * *

Sharp and Carter both snapped their heads up and looked at each other. A scream. Carter's eyes were huge, and he gasped.

Sharp pulled out his gun, disengaged the safety, and ordered Carter away. "Get back. Far back. And don't come out until I call for you."

Carter's head quickly moved up and down as he backed away. He turned and fled back in the direction of the ATV.

Sharp headed toward the barn, about fifty yards away. He set to quickly checking the perimeter of the barn, moving as stealthily as mud, rain, darkness, age and body composition would allow. He slipped twice and fell. There were dislodged rocks and tree branches everywhere. The falls were inconvenient and infuriating, but he was not injured.

He stopped near the window and stood for a moment to listen, and to catch his breath. He heard whimpering followed by a deep sigh and groan of satisfaction. His stomach turned, and a breath rushed into his lungs. Launching off his back leg, he propelled himself forward without further checking his path. He was panicking. He tripped over a rock and lost his balance, colliding with the wall of the barn, causing a clatter.

* * *

As he finished, Keres heard something outside the barn which sparked his alarm. He jumped up and threw his pants and boots on, grabbed his gun, and cocked it. He aimed at the spot on the wall from where the noise came and fired twice.

He threw his shirt over his head and as soon as his arms were through the sleeves, threw his coat over. He was going to have to make a run for it.

He held the gun at the ready as he approached the exit.

A disorienting crash from outside the door sent splinters and fragments of rotten wood across the room. A rapid succession of bullets flew from Keres's pistol into the night. He fled.

* * *

Luck was the only factor in Sharp's continued existence. When he bent down to pick up a rock big enough to bust the rotting door in, two shots missed him by inches.

He managed to wrestle a large stone from the ground, and in his best attempt at an Olympic level stone throw, he lobbed it through the door, then hit the ground and rolled away, to avoid the creation of any further, unnecessary holes in his body. It was the right call. A shower of bullets flew through the space he occupied only a moment before, followed by furious, racing footsteps.

Keres was getting away.

Sharp picked himself up and in a split second decision, chose to follow the son of a bitch. *That bastard is gonna pay for what he did.* He held up his flashlight to get an idea of the landscape, and took off running as fast as he could, as nearly as he could tell, following the fleeing man. It felt like he was moving in slow motion, though to an outside observer, his speed and dexterity would have been impressive. Until he face-planted directly into a hole the size of a grave.

"God *dammit!*" he screamed; certain he was alone.

But he wasn't.

As he scurried to climb out of the grave, blind in the darkness and in a hurry, he missed the man standing over him. When he placed his hands outside the hole and began to lift himself out, he felt the barrel of a gun press against his forehead.

"Ah-ah-ah. I don't think so."

* * *

Carruthers and his team hit the ground running. At the distance they'd been dropped, and considering the conditions, they'd have about a six minute run to reach the barn. The sound of wind, pouring rain, and persistent rolling thunder overpowered the noise of the helicopter shortly after it was out of sight.

Nearing the barn, the perimeter and sniper teams began to branch from the core group. Each man moved toward his planned locations, but after hearing a rapid succession of gunfire, every member of the team scattered for cover.

A few moments passed before the next frenzy of movement unfolded around the barn. Frantic whispers were heard through radio transmissions as the officers assembled around the barn, setting up their posts around the area.

The breaching team leader reported to Carruthers over the radio, "The entry is already breached. Hostage is inside but in an altered state. The assailant is not present."

"Sending tactical medicine in," he responded. With a brief nod, the medic descended on the barn.

* * *

The clatter of a heavy object colliding with and breaking something nearby filled Mitch's head. It sounded hollow, like old wood shattering and raining down onto the ground. Everything sounded far away, but somehow loud at the same time.

The roar of gunfire... *was* it gunfire? Two loud booms, a moment of silence, then another stream of explosive pops filled his head. *He found me. I knew he'd figure it out.* Mitch remembered a series of events unfolding almost the same way, a memory of his traumatic childhood being relived.

His arms and legs were bound, his eyes covered, his body violated. The images in his mind were unclear behind the floating haze of... what in the hell was he on? His voice was thick and raw, courtesy of drugs and screaming. "Jim..." He didn't recognize his own groggy, prolonged plea.

It'll be over soon. Jim found me again. Thank you, God.

Mitch tried moving his head to get the blindfold off and raising his limbs, but couldn't do either. He was still stuck. Still in the dark. He listened, but no one was there. He was still alone. His stomach sank into the deepest pit of despair. *What if no one was here? What if I'm hallucinating? Did I imagine the noises?* Tears spilled from his eyes, and were absorbed by the blindfold, leaving it saturated with his agony.

I'm gonna die here.

Footsteps smacked loudly on the ground around the mattress as what sounded like an entire army of men gathered around. He heard a man's voice. *Oh, God. Is he coming back? Is this it? Is he going to kill me this time?* "No!" he shrieked. The same way he had as a boy. "Please... no more."

131

* * *

Kahrren gasped and grabbed Bub's arm. Her grasp was tight as she leaned into him. He scooped her up with his giant arms. She grabbed at her head. "Oh, my god."

"What's wrong, Miss? Are you hurt?"

"Sharp's in trouble."

Bub turned and conquered the short distance to the idling helicopter faster than an olympic sprinter and set her down on the closest seat. *"Stay. Here."* He used his most authoritative voice and Kahrren was in no shape to argue.

Kahrren pressed her temples and squeezed her eyes in an effort to relieve the vice-like pain in her head. By the time she opened her eyes, Bub was gone. She pulled her legs up and bent her head forward, resting her splitting head on her bent knees.

A whirl of sounds and emotions bombarded her mind. No matter how hard she tried to focus, to ground herself, she couldn't keep outside information from getting in. She was picking up thoughts from everyone out there. *Mitch, Sharp, Bub, Carruthers... Who the fuck is Carter? And Enoch Keres.*

She dug her fingers into the back of her head and neck. Somehow it helped the pain and allowed her to focus. *Keres has Sharp. A cliff. And a murderous intent.*

"Brittany!" she screamed, hoping against hope the girl's spirit would be able to hear her. She repeated the scream, trying to project her thoughts like she did early when silently communicating with Bub. She briefly looked at the pilot, who seemed not to hear her over the noise of the helicoptor and storm. She saw him pressing the headphones into his ears, listening intently.

"Why all the yelling? Oh, shit. What's wrong with you?" Brittany's flippant attitude changed when she saw Kahrren's pallor and pain-induced grimace. "God, Kahrren, are you okay?"

"Sharp is in trouble. Bub is going after him, but he doesn't know where he should be."

"I'm on it." Brittany disappeared.

Kahrren, never having been one for waiting around no matter how poorly her condition, stood and moved forward the short distance to the cockpit. She tapped the pilot on the shoulder, waited for him to remove his headset, and asked if he had a radio.

"Of course I do. But you can't interfere—"

"I have no intention of interfering. *You* are going to get on that radio and find someone called Carter who is in this area. And you're going to do it *now*."

"And exactly who do you think *you* are?"

Kahrren abruptly leaned in and went face to face with the pilot, rage-screaming a command from her mind to his, *Do it now!*

The man startled and grabbed the radio, all color having left his face. He fiddled with the knob, avoiding the channels being used for the operation until he found the young man.

"This is Carter. Identify yourself."

Kahrren grabbed the radio from the man with one swift motion. "My name is Kahrren. I am here as a consultant to help find Detective Adams. Are you the one who brought Sharp up here? With the buggy?"

"Yes, the ATV."

"Yeah, one of those. I need you to get over here and pick me up. I gotta get over to the cliff they're heading toward so I can be closer to what's going on. And I can't do it by myself."

"I don't think it's such a good idea, miss. I think you should st—"

"I don't give two shits what you think. Get in that vehicle and get over here!"

The pilot grabbed the radio from Kahrren's hand. "Get back and don't try that again. I won't put up with any more of your little stunts. You won't be interfering with this operation. Sit down and be quiet." He keyed the radio. "Sorry about that, Carter. Won't happen again."

She puffed out her cheeks then emitted a grunty yell as she turned and moved away. Without bothering to stop, she headed straight off the chopper and toward the cliff. The terrain was rougher than she'd anticipated making her wish she'd brought her cane.

She had to stop multiple times to check her surroundings with the flashlight on her phone, and to focus on picking up thoughts from Keres or Sharp to follow where they were headed. Her progress was frustratingly slow. She sat to take a break from her treacherous journey. Pain shot through her like lightning, hot and intense.

She was surprised a few moments later to hear the buzzing growl of an ATV not too far away. She stood and pulled her phone out of her pocket. She turned the back of the phone toward the noise and turned her flashlight on and off several times in quick succession.

The ATV headed her direction and stopped a few feet short of where she stood. "Are you Kahrren?"

She genuinely smiled. "That's me."

"I'm Carter. May I help you into the *buggy*?"

"Oh, ha ha. But yes. I am not exceedingly nimble these days."

"My pleasure." He was out of the ATV faster than seemed humanly possible and had her situated in no time.

"How'd you know where to find me?"

"Well, when I showed up at the Blackhawk, you were nowhere to be found, and there's only one cliff in this area, so I headed for it."

"You mean I'm headed the right direction?"

"As a matter of fact, you are. I am not sure how, because this is a really bad area, but you made it really far."

"Must be magic."

"I guess so. Let's go." He pointed the vehicle the right direction and headed for the cliff. Arriving a short distance from the cliff he shut down the engine and looked at Kahrren. "We're gonna have to walk from here."

* * *

Mitch heard a voice speak softly to him. "Detective Adams, I'm Sergeant Stevens. Next to me is our medic, Shadman. I'm going to cover you with a blanket, then I'll remove your blindfold, okay?"

Mitch moved his head in a shallow nod. "Get me out of here." He heard his voice, deep, slow, slurred, and very hoarse. The blanket was warm as it draped over his body. His shoulders and ankles were exposed, but nothing more. The blindfold was pulled up from his eyes so deftly he didn't even feel the man's hands. Stevens said, "Okay, I'm going to release your arms and legs, one by one."

"Please just do it as fast as possible. I need to get out of here." Nimble movements preceded his liberation from the restraints. He turned over into a seated position, holding up his wobbly frame with one arm and the blanket tightly to his body with the other. Despite the sense of relief that washed over him, he could not stop clutching the blanket which served as the only sense of protection. He looked around at the men. "Where's Jim?"

Stevens was still kneeling next to the mattress as the breach team exited the barn. Only the medic remained with him. "He went after your attacker."

Mitch nodded. "Mind if I get on the gurney myself? I don't want to be pawed at any more, if it's all the same to you." At least, that's what he tried to say.

Shadman knelt at the edge of the mattress as Stevens moved back. "That should be okay when it's time to move you but I'd like to check you out first." He showed Mitch his small flashlight. "I won't touch you if I can avoid it." Seeing his nod, Shadman flashed the light into Mitch's eyes to check for pupillary reaction. Explaining each step, he managed to check him over thoroughly enough to ascertain that moving to the gurney on his own would be fine.

* * *

Sharp was exhausted, but with a gun in his back, he had no choice but to keep going. "I need to rest."

"Shut your mouth and keep moving." Keres jammed the gun deeper into Sharp's ribs. "We're almost there."

"Almost where?"

Keres responded with another jab at Sharp's side. "Move."

While Sharp was beyond exhausted from the long hours he'd been working, the stress of a missing partner, and the arduous journey through the woods, he was still deliberately walking at a slower pace than he was able, in hopes that the delay would allow responding officers to timely arrive. He even took a few good tumbles by purposely overcorrecting when he began to slip.

Sharp saw the cliff from a distance. "What do you think is gonna happen? How are you going to escape from here?"

"Keep going."

Sharp took two more steps and dropped to his knees and fell forward onto his hands. "Please. Not like this. I can't stand heights."

"God, you're worse than *he* is." He nodded in the direction of the barn. "God damned crybabies."

"Is he still alive?"

"He was when I left him."

Sharp lifted his hands off the ground and sat back on his heels, resting on his knees. "Why couldn't you just leave him alone? You did enough damage to him when he was a kid."

"Same reason you're going over the cliff. I don't like unfinished business." He waved with his weapon hand from Sharp to the cliff edge.

The action gave Sharp the opportunity he was waiting for to grab the gun in his ankle holster. He whipped his left leg up and pulled up on his pants leg in a swift motion. He grabbed his pistol with his right hand, raised it, and fired.

Keres fired his own gun on the way down, hitting Sharp in the neck, well above the protection his ballistic armor provided. The shot dissected his carotid artery. Sharp crumpled to the ground in a grisly, crimson mass, grasping at his throat for the few seconds he retained consciousness, then went still.

* * *

From the treeline a woman's voice screamed, *"No!"* Kahrren rushed toward the men and fell to her knees at the fallen detective's side. "Sharp! Sharp! Come on! Don't you go. Dammit, you stay here!" She felt for a pulse on the opposite side of his neck from the bullet wound but detected nothing. If he was still breathing, she couldn't see it.

She heard a clicking noise, from a few feet away. Being the daughter of a cop, she was well acquainted with the sound of a cocking gun. She looked up at Keres who had returned to a standing position, approximately halfway between where Kahrren knelt and the cliff edge. Standing next to him, she saw the most welcome sight she could imagine.

Brittany.

She raised her hands to show Keres she was unarmed and compliant. "I'm only here for him. Run now and you may get away."

"You, my dear, are a loose end. I can't have it."

"It would be a mistake. The Chief of Police is my godfather. He'll never let you live if I die. It will only be a matter of time. And time, for you, is running out." With a pronounced effort, she slowly stood. Her eyes locked with his.

Seemingly from nowhere she started giggling.

"What the fuck is wrong with you? What are you laughing at?" Keres sounded angry.

"Do you like movies?"

"What?"

"I really like movies. Know what my favorite movies are?"

"I don't fucking care what your favorite movies are. Are you insane?"

She shrugged. "Probably." She looked to his left and wiggled her eyebrows at her supernatural friend. "But I've always liked the one with the kid who sees dead people. And *Ghost.*" She looked directly at Brittany, hoping she'd get the message. She didn't.

Keres raised his arm to take aim right at Kahrren's face.

She completely disregarded the barrel in her face. "You know, *that scene in the subway...*" It took another moment for Brittany to realize Kahrren was talking to *her*.

"Oh," Brittany drew out, walking toward Keres. *"Ghost!"* Brittany thrust her arm forward and into Keres's chest. Unable to prepare for what he could not see, he stumbled backward and spun around putting his back to the cliff. She pushed him again. He tumbled backward, dropping his gun. One final lunge forward and Brittany shoved the murderous pervert over the cliff.

Kahrren fell to her knees, panting. "Good god, Brittany, it *took* you long enough!"

"Uh... yeah. Sorry about that." She walked toward Kahrren and knelt next to her, looking down on Sharp. She smiled.

"Why are you smiling?" Kahrren's voice was soft, and surprisingly, even to her, not accusatory.

"He was a good one. He won't have any trouble at all."

"What, like going to heaven?"

"Something like that."

"You're a good one, too, Brittany. Thank you for saving me." Kahrren reached over and held her hand out for Brittany, who reached out and touched it.

"It was nice knowing you, Kahrren. I have to go now. I guess... saving you is what I was supposed to do."

"What?" Kahrren looked at Brittany's face. It was serene. "Where are you going?"

She stood up. "On." She turned toward the cliff and walked off, but instead of the fall Kahrren expected, she walked through thin air until she simply faded away.

"Well that was unexpected." Kahrren looked up to determine where the voice came from.

"Oh, for fuck's sake. Really?"

Chapter Thirteen

"Why can't you ever listen to what you're told, Miss? I swear you're going to drive me to an early grave."

Bub was fuming, but it didn't stop her from smarting off. "It won't matter. I'll still be able to talk to you and make you mad."

"Kahrren!" he shouted. *"That's enough."* His head fell backward, face to the sky. "Can't you see we have enough to deal with out here? Do you really need to add your smart ass comments and flippant attitude to all this?"

"After all these years, don't you know it's my defense mechanism? I had a gun pointed at my face and saw two men die today, one of whom I really liked. Don't you think maybe *I* am having a tough time processing all of this too?" She started to turn away but snapped back, her voice climbing in pitch and volume. *"I didn't even want to be involved in this!"* She hated rage-crying. The uncontrollable sobbing that was born of pure, intense anger was too overwhelming to hold back. "Sharp. Rodriguez. Mitchell Fucking Adams. *And you!* You all dragged me into this no matter how many times I said no. So you can take your admonishment, your disapproval, and your judgment and *shove them up your fucking ass!"* She shrieked the comment and stomped away as best she could with her bum legs and muddy footwear.

No one at the scene had ever witnessed *anyone* talking to Chief Donovan in such a way. A couple of brave souls headed toward her with the intention of intercepting. The chief held up a hand and shouted, "No. Leave her." Though visibly surprised, as well as frustrated, they halted and let her pass.

"Carter!" she croaked at the top of her lungs. "Mind if I hitch a ride with you? I'm not getting back on that helicopter."

Carter looked helplessly toward the police chief, who nodded, then looked back at Kahrren. "As long as you don't mind the cold and wet, I'd be happy to escort you out of here. It'll be a few minutes though."

"Fine." She walked on, putting as much distance between her and Bub as possible.

The ATV had carried Kahrren and Carter away from the cliff and was used again to retrieve the remains of Detective James Sharp. She headed for the vehicle which was now parked near the helicopter, which had also been relocated to a clearing only a hundred yards from the barn.

Multiple flood lights had been set up around the barn, highlighting Mitch's exodus from the barn. The medic walked next to him, asking questions, repeatedly checking vitals, and constantly prodding at him to keep him awake. Covered up to his neck with thick, woolen blankets, only his battered, sunken face was visible, even then, it was obscured by an oxygen mask.

When Kahrren saw him come out, she slowly approached, completely bypassing Bub.

"Stop," Mitch said. The medic and assisting officers slowed to a halt and made a space for Kahrren. "You saved me again?" His eyes glossed over as he looked up at her.

She nodded. "Let's not make a habit of this, huh?" She hid a sob behind a laugh, trying not to make things worse for him. *The last thing he needs is me crying over what happened.*

"Kahrren, what aren't they telling me?" His voice was soft and creaky from disuse.

She looked at the men around him. "You haven't told him?"

They shook their heads in unison. One man, identifiable by the name embroidered on his chest as Shadman, stated, "We have only talked about topics relevant to his medical condition, miss. The rest is not our place."

"Is he stable?" Kahrren asked.

Shadman nodded.

"Give us a minute." She waited for their retreat but instead saw them each looking at one another, trying to decide whether they should comply. *"Now,"* she barked. It didn't take longer than a second for them to comply. This tiny woman was fierce as hell. And equally scary.

"Mitch, Sharp never gave up trying to find you. For days, he was doing everything he could to figure out what happened to you. He made his way up here to rescue you. When he got to you he managed to chase Keres out of the cabin and out into the forest."

"Where is he now?"

Kahrren slowly shook her head, her lips parted, as she tried to find the way to tell him what happened. "After Keres held him at gunpoint and marched him toward a cliff, Sharp tried to fire at him, but Keres saw it coming and fired back. Sharp was hit in the neck and was killed almost instantly. I'm so sorry, Mitch." She stood close to him, but for his sake, as well as her own, she didn't dare reach out a hand to touch him. Neither one of them needed the more intense connection it would bring.

Mitch turned his head away and closed his eyes. "Thank you, Kahrren."

She stepped back and nodded at the medical team waiting to load him onto the waiting helicopter. It took a few minutes for them to get Mitch situated, but once he was, the medic and assisting officers moved solemnly away from the helicopter. Moving several paces away, they stood and faced each other. Every policeman in the woods, accompanied by one sole firefighter, converged, forming two parallel lines. Seeing the lines form, Kahrren moved to the end of one of them. She placed her hand over her heart as the others brought their hands up in salute. Two officers moved between the lines of men, escorting the remains of their fallen comrade toward the ramp. It was a display worthy of the hero he was.

* * *

It took about an hour of argument, a supervised drive, and an intervention by Andrew, for Kahrren to convince Lorna that she was up to a couple of short errands on her own. But the autonomy felt good. After all, it had been almost six months since suffering her injuries, and she had fought damn hard to recover.

After parking, she pawed through her purse to find her blue placard, allowing access to the handicap accessible parking spots. Feeling grateful to be able to use these spots, she was nevertheless determined to give back the sign at some point. The sooner, the better.

An exotic looking woman with luxurious, velvety hair registered Kahrren at the visitor's check-in. Adorned with a fancy new paper bracelet identifying her as a visitor, clearly the height of fashion, Kahrren found her way to the elevator.

She pressed the button for the fourth floor and stood next to an extraordinarily peaceful-feeling man. She closed her eyes and listened to a chorus of Gregorian chants spilling from his mind. Either he was extremely guarded, or he was the most focused person she'd ever encountered. The melody was so beautiful she found herself wholly lost in it. Not realizing they'd reached her stop, she came back to herself after hearing the gentle clearing of his throat.

"I beg your pardon. I was somewhere else. Thank you." She stepped off the elevator and turned to smile at him. He smiled very pointedly back and pressed the button to close the door.

The fourth floor hadn't changed at all since she was a patient there six months before. She walked down the corridor to the nurse's station.

Before she could say anything, she heard, "Bless my soul, I didn't expect to see you back here this soon!" It was a voice with which she was entirely familiar from her own stay at the hospital. Her favorite nurse.

"I never thought I'd be back, but thankfully I'm just visiting. How are you, Linda?"

"If I was any better, I'd have to be twins. It's good to see you, sweetie. Are you staying out of trouble?"

"Nope."

"I didn't think you would. But don't you land yourself back in here. I don't need any more gray hair from your sass."

"Yes, ma'am. I'll do my best. Can you remind me where room 418 is?"

"I sure can. But you better be ready for some nastiness. He is grumpy today." Linda pointed down the hall. "Go straight down the hall, don't turn at the desk. Keep going. It's the one that looks like it should have been a janitor's closet, but they stuck a room number on the door. You'll know when you see it."

"Thank you. You take care."

"Mmhmm. You too, honey."

Kahrren's trip down the hall was as eventful as she expected. She picked up on sadness, anger, relief, even some joy. She did her best to remain focused but the task was difficult. The hospital was not an easy place to be with her ability, especially since it was getting stronger by the day.

She knocked on the door, which was mostly closed. Her knock pushed it open a bit. Another familiar face greeted her. A mop of wavy black hair came into view first. His lovely tawny skin framed his kind, nearly black eyes. As he leaned around the door his expression morphed quickly from curious to baffled. "Miss McClintock, I did not expect to see you here. Are you well?"

She smiled and shook his outstretched hand. "It's good to see you Dr. Patel. I am doing quite well, thank you. How's our friend here?" she asked, nodding toward Mitch.

"Oh, I'll let him tell you about it. I was about to finish up here. It was lovely to see you."

"And you. Have a nice day." Dr. Patel exited the room and closed the door. Kahrren turned to Mitch. "So, two days in. Are you bored out of your mind?"

"How did you do this for all those weeks?" He elevated his voice when he said it, but she wasn't sure he was joking.

"I had a lot of drugs." She moved to the chair next to his bed and sat. "Besides, I'm not sure we can count the first week since I was unconscious almost the whole time."

"I'd kill to be unconscious. This place sucks. They won't let me get up and do anything."

"I'm so sorry, Mitch. I didn't realize you were so badly injured."

"Well, I don't think it's as bad as they say. I have some injuries, but I think they want to keep me from going to psych." He rolled his eyes.

"Yeah. Therapy blows."

"You've been in therapy?"

"Oh, yeah. Since I got out of the hospital. Physical *and* psychological. Evidently I have trouble processing emotionally difficult situations and use sarcasm to cope."

"Duh."

"I know, right?" She shifted to get more comfortable. "I hated when people asked how I was…"

"I completely agree with *that*."

"So, how about… is there anything you'd like to tell me?"

"I'd think you, of all people, would know I don't want to talk about what happened."

"I definitely understand." She placed her elbow on the arm of the chair and leaned on it to support herself. "But that's not really what I was asking. I already know as much as I want to about what happened. What I was trying to ask is whether there is anything you'd like to get off your chest? I always complained about the food and how freaking uncomfortable the bed was." She paused, allowing time for him to comment, but he just waited for her to get on with it. "And how there's never anything good on TV."

"Well, you're right about all of those things. The food, the bed, and the entertainment are all terrible. One out of five stars. Would not recommend."

Kahrren nodded and waited. Several silent minutes went by, but she was as stubborn as he was. Maybe even more so. "So, I'm not leaving for a while. I finally got Lorna to let me out of the house by myself. You're stuck with me."

"I really don't have anything to tell you."

"Okay." She grabbed the remote and started flipping through the channels. "It's one o'clock. Time for my favorite cooking show."

He actually smiled. "It's the only one worth watching."

They watched the entire episode in silence. Well, Mitch did. Kahrren was being pestered by her new companion, one recently deceased James Sharp.

Tell him I don't regret it.

Tell him to contact my lawyer about the will.

Tell him everything is going to be okay.

Tell him, Rodriguez wants him to go back to work as soon as he's ready.

Tell him...

Tell him...

Tell him...

"So do you have any questions for me?" Kahrren finally asked. She made a silly face and added, "I remember how much you liked knowing every little thing when *I* was the one in here."

"Yeah, actually. Did you ever play the quiet game when you were little?" His chest started to rise and fall rapidly. She jumped out of the chair and practically flung herself over the bedside until she heard him laugh.

"Mitch! You complete shit. I thought you were having a seizure or something." She groaned and plopped back in her chair.

He only laughed harder.

She waved her hand at him in playful disregard.

"Rude," she commented in a soft grumble.

Most of the afternoon passed with light chatter and inane commentary about the sad state of modern television shows. Kahrren placed her hands on her knees and said, "Well, I'd better get going. I have to stop by the station to see Rodriguez."

"What for?"

She grinned. "I'm going to bill the department for my involvement as a consultant."

"How very resourceful of you."

"I believe in working with what you have." She put on her coat and picked up her handbag. "How long do you think you'll be in here?"

"About a week, they said."

"Would you mind if I visit again?"

"Will it be like this?"

"Probably."

"Then yeah, it would be fine. But there's one condition."

"Which is?

"Please bring me better food."

"Ha! I told you it was bad." She walked over to the bed near his legs. "Is it okay if I do something?" She reached her hand indicating she wanted to touch him.

"Not a psychic something."

"Not a psychic something, I promise." He lifted his hand, gesturing his permission.

Kahrren took the pillow from where it lay next to his legs on the bed, removed it from its pillow case and set the pillow back down, still holding the case. She tied a knot in the middle of the open end and the closed end, then picked up the pillow again. She rolled it tightly, lengthwise and slid it back in the pillow case forming a makeshift bolster. "Lift." She tapped his knees and waited for him to obey, then slid the rolled pillow under his knees to elevate them and take the pressure off his lower back. The massage therapist in her lived on.

"Oh, that's so much better," he said. "Thanks."

"You're welcome, Mitch. See ya tomorrow."

"See ya."

She walked into the corridor and started toward the elevator.

"Hey, Kahrren?" Mitch hollered from his room.

"Yeah?" She reappeared and leaned on the door frame, then waited for him to vocalize his question.

"Did Sharp say anything to you about me?"

"He did."

Mitch's face started to redden, and she could feel the tension rise in him.

"He asked me to make sure you're taken care of."

* * *

146

Parking on the street in front of the police station was almost impossible. Kahrren had to circle the block four times before something opened up. The city had come back to life over the last couple of days as its residents saw the skies begin to clear.

As she walked into the station, she gripped her cane tightly, stopping to rest a couple of times along the way. Though she had begun to feel stronger, the combination of traipsing through the forest like a commando and being around the psychic energy of as many people as one finds in a hospital and a police station, each took their toll.

Her fingers rapped gently on Rodriguez's door, which was only half closed. "Knock, knock."

"Well, Miss McClintock. I wasn't expecting to see you today. Is everything okay?" He pulled out a chair for her and returned to his seat.

Kahrren sat and placed her handbag in her lap. "Yes, thank you, Lieutenant. Things being what they are, I am doing fine." She pulled an envelope out of her bag and leaned forward to hand it to him. "Chief Donovan said I should give this to you."

He reached his hand out to take it. "What is this?"

"It's my invoice for consulting."

The low grumble which emanated from his chest rolled into a hearty laugh. "Is that so? And who said you were going to be a *paid* consultant?"

"That would be the chief of police." Her voice was honey as she lifted her cell phone. "I can get him on the line if you need to hear it directly from him."

He tapped his fingers dramatically on the desk. "You are something else, you know?" He shook his head as his face widened, presenting a sea of dazzling, white teeth. "I'll get this processed. It'll take a couple of days."

"Great. I'll ca—"

"On one condition." He pulled the bill out of the envelope and looked it over. His jaw went slack and he squinted moving the paper closer and further from his face. "Miss McClintock, are you sure you don't have the decimal point in the wrong place?"

"Gee, I don't know, Lieutenant. Why don't we ask some of your *other* psychic consultants if they think my fee is too high?"

Smirking, he raised his hands in surrender. "Point taken. You drive a hard bargain, young lady." He tossed the paper on his desk and sat back in his chair, folding his hands over his abdomen. "But the only way I'll agree to pay this is if you agree to make yourself available to us in the future."

"Wait. You want me to keep doing this?"

"Yes, as we need you."

"Do I get a gun?"

"Absolutely not." He leaned forward and folded his hands on the desk. "You get money. That'll have to be enough."

"Fine. But I get autonomy. No schedules, I work from home unless *I* believe I need to be at a crime scene, or any other location. It's up to me. And I want a contract."

"Fine. I'll draw up a contract." He paused, appearing to consider something. "Is there any chance you'd agree to carry the title private investigator? We'll pay for you to get licensed. There's a test you'd have to pass later on."

"I can agree to those terms. It'll look better on paper, am I right?"

"Yes. It's difficult to explain a psychic consultant. No one blinks at a PI."

"Do I get to work with Mitch?"

"Yes. If he comes back. But you won't be working exclusively with him. Other detectives will need your help."

"And how, pray tell, will you explain my ability to people who don't already know?"

"Well, let's worry about it when we get there. For now if there's something you can't explain, you tell me, I'll tell them."

"All right. That seems workable. Thanks, Lieutenant. I expected a check and got a job. I'll consider it a win." She paused, then said, "There's one more thing."

"And what would that be?"

"Do you know if anyone is collecting funds for Sharp's services? If so, I'd like to make a donation."

"It seems Sharp already had everything taken care of. The only thing left is when it will take place. I will let you know as soon as we have the details."

He stood and held the door for her. "Have a nice day."

"You, too." She rose with the assistance of her cane and slowly made her way back down to her car.

She strapped in and started the engine, then grabbed her phone and started pounding out a text to Lorna.

Kahrren: Got a job with the cops. On my way home. Need anything?

Lorna: WT actual F? How did that happen? Yes. Bring dinner.

Kahrren: Sure. Explain when I get there. Pizza?

Lorna: Sounds good. Drive carefully. Salad. Breadsticks. Soda.

Kahrren: Not my first rodeo. Be home soon.

* * *

She walked into the townhouse with two bags, heading straight for the kitchen. She set them on the counter and turned to Lorna and Andrew who were enjoying the day's final cup of coffee at the table. "With all this stuff, I couldn't carry the pizza too. Would anybody mind going out to get it? I'm beat."

Andrew rose. "Of course. Back in a flash." He stepped to the entryway, slipped on some shoes, and went out the door. He wasn't joking. He returned carrying the pizza in less than a minute. "This smells great."

Lorna popped up and began unloading the bags Kahrren had carried in and setting the table for their meal. "Kahrren, you look tired. Please sit. We'll do this."

Kahrren nodded her thanks and made it over to the kitchenette, taking her regular seat. "So, I took the invoice to Rodriguez. He is going to pay me. But there's a condition."

Lorna and Andrew stopped and faced Kahrren, waiting for her to continue. Lorna looked like she was ready for a fight.

"I agreed to continue consulting for the police. And I'm going to get a private investigator's license, which they are going to pay for."

Lorna brightened. *"That's* the job you mentioned? Being a police consultant?"

"Yup. I'm getting a contract and everything. *Plus*, I told him that I work when *I* say, and I work from home unless *I* deem it necessary to go to a crime scene."

"Kahrren, how great! I'm so glad you included those caveats. This could actually work out pretty well for you." Lorna placed plates, napkins, and cups on the table, then leaned down and hugged Kahrren. "Are you sure you're up to it though?"

"Well, that's the beauty of it. I do feel up to it, but I have a built-in failsafe of not having to go do anything if I can't manage it. It's entirely up to me."

Andrew carried several food items and placed them on the table, then sat. "That is really great, Kahrren. And he agreed to pay you the rate you put on the invoice?"

"Yep. But he did verify I hadn't misplaced a decimal."

"Wow. Fantastic. Congratulations." He patted her shoulder, grinning. "If I'm not mistaken, you'll likely make more than when you were massaging." He set to work pouring soda for each of them

"It's a strong possibility. I have come to realize as my recovery continues that I won't be going back to my career. While it makes me very sad, it is what it is. At least I have this opportunity now. So, it's something."

"It sure is. Here's to Kahrren's new gig. May it be both manageable and prosperous." Andrew held his soda glass up and clinked it against the others.

"Hear, hear!" Lorna added.

They devoured their meal and settled in to watch a movie before retiring for the evening.

Chapter Fourteen

One week later

Car after car slowly rolled in procession under an unseasonably sunny sky. Practically every law enforcement and first responder vehicle from the Portland metro area and Southwest Washington, and dozens who came from across the nation showed up to honor their fallen comrade.

It took well over thirty minutes for the line of cars to pass by any one location, past crowds of civilian onlookers and people who had been touched by Sharp's actions in some way, and a sea of people who never knew who he was but came to honor a man of service. Hundreds of flags waved in the breeze, clutched by people lined up to say goodbye.

Kahrren took a seat in a spot marked with her name in the tented area of the cemetery. The chairs to her sides were reserved for Mitch to her left, and Bub to her right. Rodriguez was assigned the seat next to Bub.

As far as Kahrren's circle of friends, Lorna, Andrew, Katie, and Beth all joined the attendees standing behind the ocean of uniforms. They insisted on being there to show their gratitude and respect for one of the men who saved Kahrren's life.

Rodriguez arrived in the row and nodded a greeting to Kahrren. She smiled politely at him and returned to looking at the program which was handed to her by an usher on her arrival. By the time she was finished reading its contents, most people had found a place from which to watch the ceremony.

Next to him was Dr. Arnold Bauer, the chief medical examiner, and Sharp's best friend, accompanied by his wife, Miranda.

Bub stood in his capacity as chief near the pulpit, in preparation for his contribution as the first speaker. He looked toward Kahrren, holding her eyes for a moment before looking down and getting a hold of his face, which had begun to crack.

At the very last moment before the invocation, Mitch made his way under the tent and took his seat. Kahrren didn't have to look at him, much less touch him, to feel the grief rolling off of him, and sadly, the embarrassment he felt, knowing that most of the people here knew what had happened to him.

Her head was already swimming with the torrent of thoughts and emotions emanating from such a massive crowd of people. Sitting with her legs crossed, her hands were squeezing each other so tightly, all of the color had gone from her fingers and she was shaking.

As Bub's voice began to resonate from the giant sound system, she used it as a point of focus in an attempt to keep her head straight.

"I am Chief of Police, Robert Donovan. I'd like to thank you all for joining us in celebrating this man, who spent his life in service to our city." He invited Arnie to the microphone to lead an invocation.

Arnie's anguished voice was soft, and he did not waste any time with superfluous speech. He offered his thanks, asked for a blessing over the proceedings, and got the hell off the stage as fast as he could. He nodded to Chief Donovan who returned to the microphone as an echo of amens filled the air.

"James William Sharp was a man of courage and dedication. He was a man who made a difference in thousands of lives in this city. It is true he was known for being a little acerbic, and a little impatient. I believe it was because he expected of other people what he gave, himself; his very best. And he had no interest in waiting around for people to figure out it was expected of them too." Bub smiled at the crowd of onlookers, waiting for their laughter to subside. "I have known Jim Sharp for nearly three decades. I remember when he joined the Portland Police Department, only a short time after I did. People talked about how his wit matched his name. Sharp wit. Sharp personality. Sharp tongue. Jim was the kind of guy who was perhaps a bit difficult to like, but at the same time, a guy that everybody loved. He knew everything there was to know about being a police officer. He had a ferocious hatred of people who hurt others for their own gain. I believe it was the fuel that kept his fire burning."

Uncharacteristically, Bub's head and shoulders slumped forward. His usually flawless facade of placidity and control vanished. His chest rose and fell in uneven, jolting motions. Tears spilled down his face.

There was dead silence from the crowd. This was not the chief they were used to seeing.

His smooth bass voice quavered and cracked as he carried on. "Detective James Sharp is a man to whom I owe an enormous personal debt. He and his partner rescued my own goddaughter, the person in this world who is more precious to me than anything else, from the clutches of a man who stalked and attempted to brutally murder her. She would not be here today if he and his partner, Detective Mitchell Adams, had not given their very best at every turn, trusted their hunches, and done some of the finest detective work I have ever seen." He nodded his tortured gratitude to Mitch, who nodded back, tears streaming down his face.

Kahrren reached over, gently squeezed Mitch's hand, and looked at him. He looked back and placed his arm around her. She leaned into him and they quietly sobbed as Bub continued.

"The events leading to the loss of this decorated officer of the law demonstrated his dedication, his determination, and possibly... his disregard for protocol, but I don't think any of us will fault him for that." He took a moment to wipe his face. During the pause, there was a conspicuous echo of sniffles and labored gasps in an effort to control crying from the throng of mourners.

"Sharp did everything possible, *and* some seemingly impossible things, to identify and locate the man who assaulted a fellow police officer. Despite the unimaginable handicap of the recent storms, Sharp found his way through impossible circumstances, impossible terrain, and impossible odds to aid in the recovery of Detective Adams. He gave his life to save his partner. There is no braver thing I can think of. We were lucky to have James Sharp as an example. Please join me in a moment of silence to honor Detective James William Sharp."

A long minute passed. "Thank you," the chief said. He moved away from the pulpit, shook hands with the next speaker, and left the stage, finding his seat next to Kahrren. He gently tapped the arm Mitch had around Kahrren's shoulders and replaced it with his own. "Thank you, Detective Adams."

Kahrren kept hold of Mitch's hand and squeezed tightly as Bub pulled her into a crushing one-armed embrace, then finally eased. Mitch made no attempt to pull away. They stayed entwined listening to the rest of the speakers, all of whom had funny or impressive stories to tell about their experiences working with Sharp.

Bub nodded to his aide who spoke softly into a cell phone. Bub stood, pulling Kahrren with him. Mitch, Rodriguez, Arnie, and Miranda all stood, prompting everyone to rise and form ranks, arms up in salute. A moment later a female radio dispatcher was heard over the silent crowd.

"Radio to PD504." A brief pause laid heavy in the air. "Radio to PD504." The dispatcher waited for a response. "PD501, unable to raise PD504."

A male voice responded, "10-4. PD504 is 10-7."

A series of tones sounded. The female dispatcher followed. "All units be advised: PD504, Detective First Class James William Sharp is 10-7. His watch ended Wednesday, September 22nd. Rest in peace, Detective Sharp."

A whirlwind of activity saw the official ceremony come to a close. A reception followed at a fancy hotel downtown for the first responders and friends in attendance. By the end of the evening, Kahrren's head was swimming in other people's thoughts and emotions. And not a small amount of tequila. She was not alone in the latter.

* * *

After feeding and giving some much deserved attention to Fred, Kahrren showered and made herself ready for the day. Having spent a quiet week at home after the funeral, she was ready to head out into the world again.

Cindy and Mason mauled her with affection when she entered the brick-walled lobby of Thrive for her therapy appointments. They had settled on taking turns as her massage therapist so they could aid in her recovery.

"It's so good to be back. Last week was a monster and I am in desperate need of my therapy. The last few weeks have been hellish."

Cindy nodded in agreement. "We missed being here. It was unreal out there. We were shut down for the whole week of the storms. Then we saw you had cancelled your next few appointments, and we got worried. Is everything okay?"

"A friend passed away, and another has been in the hospital. I was helping out with some stuff. Things are getting back to normal now."

"Good," Mason added. "Now I think you'd better go. The new physical therapist is really bitchy about tardiness."

"Occupational therapist," Cindy corrected.

"The new physical therapist can cram it up her cramhole."

"I'll be sure to do that. In a timely fashion. When I don't have someone waiting on me." Kahrren turned to face the speaker, ready for a fight. "Hi, Kahrren."

"Katie! What the hell?" Kahrren leaned forward on her cane. "What are you doing here?"

"Well, I wanted to keep it a secret until I started. I only needed a few more credits to get into an occupational therapy credential program. So, I went back to school and got it done, then sailed right through the program. I'm part of the Thrive family now."

"You are so sneaky. I never even suspected."

"I'm very good at keeping secrets. Now, let's get to it. I don't want your other appointments to start late. You have lots on your agenda today."

Kahrren made her way to the gym and started her physical therapy, spent the following hour in talk therapy, received her chiropractic adjustment, then headed for the massage. It was great to get back to a normal routine.

And even better to be able to do all of it without having to disrupt Lorna's entire day.

She was ravenous when she was finished, so she stopped at a drive-thru for a bite before heading to pick up her check from Rodriguez.

When she exited the elevator, she saw something that stopped her dead in her tracks. "Mitch! You're here!" She made her way over to him. "I wasn't expecting you."

"What can I say? I'm full of surprises." She wanted him to smile to show some levity, but he only quickly lifted his eyebrows. "What are *you* doing here?"

"I am collecting my paycheck. We're sort of co-workers now."

"I beg your pardon?" His bewilderment was so pronounced it became comical.

She laughed. "I am officially a consultant for PPD."

"God save us." This time he did smile.

"I think you and I are doing pretty well as each other's saviors. And apart from one minor conflict, we work well together."

"I suppose we do. But I am on the desk until I am cleared by some paper pusher to get back in the field. So I guess you'll be working with Humpty and Dumpty over there." He looked sideways at Daniels and Wynn, who was eyeing Kahrren as she talked to Adams. "Looks like Dumpty has an eye on you."

Kahrren whipped her head around and caught him gawking at her. "*Yes?*" she demanded.

His head pulled back in a jerking motion. She thought he was going to panic and stumble his words, but she was surprised. "Well, the typical order is one person asks a question, then the other gives an answer but since you're so eager to say yes, how's eight o'clock?"

Kahrren squinted as one side of her mouth came up, reminiscent of Elvis. If he was having a stroke.

"Does your mommy know you're talking to girls?" She sniped the response at him loudly so everyone could hear. Her jab was appreciated by everyone in earshot, soliciting a rumble of soft laughter. Wynn playfully grabbed at his chest, pretending to pull a dagger from his heart. "You wound me."

"You're young. You'll recover."

Daniels nudged Wynn with an elbow. "That's the chief's goddaughter. And she is kind of scary in her own right. Tread carefully."

Kahrren turned back to Mitch. "Who's the toddler?"

"New detective. Working with Daniels, I guess. For now."

"Someone ought to talk to him about biting off more than he can chew."

"Nah. We'd prefer to see him squirm," he stated confidently on behalf of his fellow lawmen.

"So, Lorna and I would like you to come to dinner. Will you come?"

"I don't know, Kahrren…"

"It's a safe place. All appropriate conversation. And lots of delicious food. Possibly even a movie or some games. Good clean fun."

"Lorna made you invite me, didn't she?"

"There's a reason you're a detective, my friend. She told me not to take no for an answer. And to find out what you like to eat."

He was quiet for a moment, riffling papers around his desk. "Nachos. Extra jalapeños. And I like cards better than board games."

"Tonight?"

"Seven."

She nodded and started to make her way to Rodriguez's office. She heard a grumble from Wynn's thoughts. *Oh, sure. Go with the exceptionally handsome and fit, age appropriate guy who saved your life. I see how it is.* The touch of a smile lifted one corner of her mouth.

She knocked on the lieutenant's officer door before poking her head in. "Hey, boss. I'm here for money and promises."

"Do you ever call first?"

"Now, why do you always have to destroy all the fun?"

"It's just how I like it. It's a fun-free zone. Come in and sit. I have both your check and your contract." He picked up the file folder sitting to his left and opened it. "It's your lucky day. We have some tax paperwork for you to fill out too." He laid the papers in front of her and placed a pen on top of them. She picked up the check and placed it in her wallet, then set to work filling out the paperwork. She very carefully read the contract before signing it.

"I'm surprised to see the contract meets my requirements. I was expecting to have to ask for revisions."

"I thought I'd save myself some trouble and have the revisions done before you showed up. It's far easier giving them orders than dealing with your wrath."

"This is why we're gonna get along so well. Am I supposed to call you LT? Loo? Boss? Like, how does this work?"

"Lieutenant is fine. Sir, if you want. Boss is okay if we're not in an official meeting with my subordinates or superiors."

"Okay, then. I'll be Kahrren, or Ms. McClintock if we're fancy." She made sure both copies of the contract were exactly the same, and signed both, then slid them to Rodriguez for his mark.

"Welcome aboard. We'll be in touch. Please keep your ringer on."

"Yup. You got it." She collected her papers and placed them in her over the shoulder messenger bag, then rose with the assistance of her cane. "Be seeing you."

"Stay safe, Ms. McClintock. I have no interest in explaining to my boss's boss's boss's boss what happened to you when you get in trouble. Ever. Again."

She smiled and gave him a mock salute with her index and middle fingers extended, moving forward from her temple.

Having departed the station, she headed for her last errand, the financial office at the hospital. She found a handicap parking spot and hanged her placard over the rearview mirror.

Moving toward the office, she walked past the elevator vestibule, and faintly heard in her mind a chorus of monks chanting. She looked around and didn't see anyone. Weird.

The sounds of hospital administration bounced around the first floor hallway as she walked down it.

Explaining to the young man at the desk why her bill was wrong, and why she believed she was being overcharged was a chore and a half. First he seemed not to understand what she meant. Then he denied the tens of thousands of dollars she was being overcharged was inaccurate.

"Young man, the surgery for which I have been double billed only occurred one time, not twice, and certainly not twice on the same day. I can promise you, they only drilled into my head one time on that day, and not again thereafter." He began to protest, but she cut him off with expert precision. "*Now*, how likely do you think it is I am actually wrong about how many times I have had a surgeon hack open my head to access my brain?"

His face was red and blotchy, and he was trying his best to bore another hole straight through her skull. He sat back in his chair and crossed his arms, completely closing himself off from reasonable conversation.

"I think I would like to talk to your supervisor. Please go get him or her for me."

"She's not available," he snapped.

Kahrren was losing her patience in the most rapid manner. As much as she wanted to telepathically shriek at him, instead she opted for actual shrieking. She stood and bellowed as best she could, despite her still crackly voice, "*I need a supervisor over here right this instant or you'll have to listen to me scream like a banshee until one arrives!*"

"Miss, please lower your voice. I am his boss, and I can help you. All you had to do was ask for a supervisor." A plump woman with a nice but long-worn skirt suit stood at the young man's side.

Kahrren looked at the young man. "Well, would you look at that…" she peered at his nametag, "Kevin! It seems there was a supervisor *when I asked for one a moment ago* after all." She turned her attention to the fifty-something woman who joined the conversation. "Thank you. I asked this young man for a supervisor, and he flatly told me there wasn't one available. It seems despite an error which will be easily verifiable with a quick medical records check, he was more concerned with being right than helping me with this rather obvious and rather expensive billing error."

"Will you please come over to my desk? I'll be glad to help you." She pointed to the seat opposite her own. She looked at poor, humiliated Kevin, and directed him to go take a break.

"Thank you. I am sure we can get this resolved in a jiffy."

"May I see your bill, please?" Kahrren handed the bill to her, as well as a copy of the list of procedures performed on the day of her surgery, which she had previously obtained. The woman, whose name plaque read Sally Witherspoon, reviewed the documents. "Oh, dear. I see what you're saying. Let me make a quick call to verify with the medical records department that they have the same information, and I can have this worked out in no time."

"Much appreciated." After less than two minutes on the phone and a few keystrokes, Kahrren's issue was resolved, and she was headed back to her car.

Arguing with the young man had not helped Kahrren's focus. She was still feeling a bit caustic and lacked the control she needed to be in such a busy venue. She was bombarded by a lightning storm of thoughts and sounds. Cries, grief, joy, worry, frustration, irritation, and nearly every other feeling found in the spectrum of human emotion.

And the super calm feeling of a man with a song in his head. This time it was Queen's "Another One Bites the Dust."

What the hell?

Chapter Fifteen

"Where are the extra jalapeños, Lorna?" Kahrren won today's battle with Lorna over helping with dinner. She felt stronger every day and was becoming confident in telling her friend to "stick it" when she was firm in her stance.

"Half the jar is on the nachos which are in the oven, half in a bowl on the table with the other toppings, and there is another jar in the refrigerator."

"You really are on top of it, aren't you? Thank you."

"I told you. I've got it and don't need your help."

In a derisive gesture Kahrren tossed her head around like some sort of demented muppet and imitated Lorna in a most unflattering way. "Meh, meh, meh, meh, I don't need your help." After she stopped laughing at her own ridiculousness, she looked at Lorna who seemed approximately halfway between disbelief and disgust if she had to judge by Lorna's crossed arms and tapping foot, with a healthy pinch of delight, as evidenced by the reluctant smile she was trying to hide.

Lorna sighed, "What do you want on your next birthday cake? You know, when you finally turn four years old, you complete child?"

"How about a unicorn? No! A honey badger." Kahrren grinned devilishly. "Because I don't give a f—"

"For heaven's sake. You are *the* most impossible person."

"You're no slouch in this arena, my dear."

"Will you please go open the door for our guest? I need a break from you for a minute."

"Aww, can't run with the big kids? Throwing in the towel?" She moved to exit the kitchen.

A kitchen towel crumpled against the back of her head, followed by Lorna's frustrated tone. "Not a bad idea, throwing the towel."

"Now who's a four year old?" Matching lingual protrusions were traded before Kahrren headed to the door, arriving just in time for Mitch's knock.

She opened the door more quickly than he seemed to be prepared for. He jolted a bit as it swung so swiftly open.

"God, did you sense me coming or something? You gotta stop doing that."

"Uh, no. Lorna saw you from the kitchen window. Sorry. Didn't mean to startle you. Come in."

"Thanks. Here, this is for you guys." He handed an extravagant bottle of tequila to Kahrren.

"My goodness. This is a lovely gift. Thank you." She closed the door and invited him to take a seat. "I'll put this in the kitchen. Would you like a drink? We've got the good hooch now!" She shook the bottle playfully.

"Maybe with dinner. Iced tea will be great for now if you have it. Or water."

"Have a seat, be comfortable. You can hang your coat there if you like." She motioned to the wall mounted board with pegs that served as their coat rack. He set his jacket over a peg and sat on the couch.

Kahrren returned with iced tea and took a seat next to him. "Here you go. Do you take sweetener or lemon?"

"No, thanks. This is perfect."

"What kind of music do you like, Mitch?"

"Well, I usually listen to music when I am working out, so house music, dance music, sometimes hip hop. But the rest of the time I am working and don't get a chance to listen to much. So I'm really not particular."

"Okay, hmm.. I think in the spirit of our fiesta style dinner, I'm going to go with one of my favorites. You're probably going to laugh but, before you do, you should know my dad used to play this when he talked about my mom."

"Got it. Sentimental favorite. No criticism."

"Good man. You understand me." She got up and went the old school route of a cassette tape. In a mere few moments Linda Ronstadt's "Canciones de Mi Padre" was pouring from the speaker.

"I've haven't heard you talk about your mom before, Kahrren."

She got pink in the cheeks and lowered her face and eyes. "I don't talk about my parents much. Not unless I'm with people I really trust."

"Aww, shucks." His grin was genuine, and he relaxed, sinking into the conversation.

"Oh, you're so funny." She rolled her eyes, all in good fun. "My dad used to put me to bed every night telling me stories about my mom or singing me songs from this album because it reminded him of her. He said she used to sing songs like these to me when she was pregnant."

"Aww, how sweet. Are these songs she grew up with? What I mean is, were they part of her culture?"

"Yes. Her grandfather was from Mexico. There's a long line of singing traditional songs on my mom's side of the family, I guess. Or there was, anyway. But they're all gone now."

"You really have no family left?"

"Nope. Dad was an only child. Mom was the only one of her siblings who made it to adulthood. I suppose there may be very distant blood relations but nobody I have ever met, or even heard of."

"I have a question."

"Sure."

"What's with the names? Your name is so unique. And you call the chief Bub. Where did those come from?"

"Well, My dad used to call the chief Bob since it's the short name for Robert—which he hated— but I couldn't pronounce it when I was little. It came out Bub, and it stuck." She pulled her knees up under her, settling in. "As for my name, it was actually mom's name, and a variation of her grandmother's before that. Well, Karren without the "H" was her grandmother's name. But she got called Karen all the time, so my mom ended up with the "H" in her name to try to get people to say it right. I can tell ya, it didn't work." Her giggle was light and happy. "My mom wanted to name me something more traditional, but, since she died during childbirth, it was left up to my dad. He chose her name to honor her."

"So, your great grandmother and your mother were a version of the same name, but what about your grandmother?"

"She was conceived right at the end of World War II. She was thusly called Victoria."

"How apropos."

"Yes, exactly. Anyway, my great-grandmother Karren married a first generation Mexican-American and started the tradition of singing songs like these to Grandma Victoria, who sang them to my mother, and... you know the rest."

"That's actually very interesting. You never know what you'll learn about people."

"That's true. Is there anything interesting you'd like to share from your family history?"

"Not really. A bunch of people married a bunch of other people. No one notable I'm aware of."

The front door opened revealing Andrew and a giant pink pastry box. "I have arrived, the festivities may begin." He gave a silly smile, and nodded Mitch's direction. "Hey, Mitch."

"Hey, Andrew. That looks promising. What did you get?"

"I found a new pastry shop and pretty much bought everything they had left because I couldn't help myself."

"I shall do my best to help ease your burden."

"Great!" Andrew disappeared into the kitchen, then poked his head out. "Looks like dinner's ready. Come on in, it's set up at the table."

Kahrren rose and headed to the kitchen with Mitch behind her. They took their seats in front of a mountain of cheese-laden tortilla chips with every possible topping one could want. Lorna and Andrew arrived at the table carrying a margarita in each hand, setting one before each plate.

"Thank you. Wow, what a set up! Do you guys eat like this all the time?" Mitch stared at the spread, not knowing precisely where to begin.

"No," Kahrren and Lorna said together.

"Yes, they absolutely do." Andrew challenged. "It may not always be this elaborate, but if it's not a pile of chips loaded with stuff, it's a super-ultra-extra topping pizza or some other culinary atrocity that mere mortals dare not consume on a regular basis."

Kahrren was trying to get every bit of a spoonful of sour cream onto her mountain of chips, shaking the spoon in a downward motion rather violently. "They also make me eat green things. Yuck."

Mitch reached over and placed his hand over Kahrren's wrist to stop her from injuring anyone with her episode. Pulling the spoon from her hand, he held it over her plate, picked up another spoon and scraped the remainder of the sour cream onto her plate. "Sharp used to say, 'Work smarter, not harder,' and I think it applies here. And green things are good for you."

Kahrren raised her nose in the air. "I like my way."

"Of course you do," Lorna said. "Because you hate being told how to do something." Lorna turned to Mitch. "Kahrren told us not to talk about what happened, but since you brought up Sharp, does that mean we can talk about him?"

A full revolution of the earth seemed to pass as she awaited his answer. His face was red and his hands shook as he balled them into a fist.

Andrew spoke up, changing the subject. "Kahrren, how did your meeting go with Rodriguez today?"

"Fine. I signed my contract and got my check. Got hit on by a teenager and went to deal with the billing thing at the hospital."

"And how did it go?"

"I got a little... "

"Bitchy?" Lorna asked.

"Yep. That's the word. I ended up talking to a supervisor and getting it worked out. So, it's done."

An uncomfortable lull in the conversation ended when Mitch spoke up. "Lorna, please forgive my rudeness. I wasn't ready for your question. If you don't mind, I don't think I'm ready to talk about it yet."

Lorna smiled with the warmth of a thousand suns. "I am the one who should apologize. I am terribly sorry. It was not my place. You have every right to be upset."

"I'm fine. And you were not out of line. It was a fair question. I did bring it up, after all. I guess I was testing the waters, not considering whether I am ready to swim yet."

Mitch and Lorna nodded at each other, a mutual acknowledgment of understanding and forgiveness.

Not one for the warm and fuzzies, Kahrren stood to cross the room, and spouted off, "Christ, I need more tequila. It's getting all ooey-gooey in here." Lorna and Andrew looked at Mitch, horrified at what his reaction would be. When Mitch erupted into a hearty belly laugh, they looked at each other, unsure at first, then followed his lead. Kahrren returned to her seat with the bottle in hand, and looked at her friends, her mouth agape in puzzlement. "What?"

This question sent them all over the edge into uncontrolled, lean-over-in-your-chair, slapping the table hysteria.

Through her wheezing, gasping laugh Lorna managed to get out, "You. Are. Such. An. *Asshole!*" Kahrren knew full well that Lorna's assessment was right. She joined in the laughter, which eventually calmed, allowing them to finish their meal without the uncertainty and unease there had been before the interaction.

They moved to the living room to play a game of *Cards Against Humanity*. Mitch was a surprisingly witty player with a depraved sense of humor. Fueled by Tequila and absent the expectations of a professional environment he let his real personality come out.

"I didn't know you were so funny, Mitch." Andrew said, at the end of another episode of roaring laughter.

"Neither did I, my friend." He grabbed his glass. "But, I suspect this has something to do with it."

"Well, I must be hilarious because I am very drunk. I think I'd better go to bed." Andrew's eyes were slowly drooping.

"I should go. It's late." Mitch started to stand and look for his phone and keys.

"No, no. You're in no shape to drive. You'll stay here." Kahrren knew it wouldn't take more than an invitation to get him to stay. His thoughts had told her so. "You'll take my room. I like sleeping right here."

"Thank you. I accept. Please show me where to go. I think I am ready for bed too."

Kahrren and Lorna quickly dressed the bed with fresh sheets and invited Mitch into the bedroom. Lorna disappeared momentarily, then returned with some loungewear for him, borrowed from Andrew's belongings. Kahrren made short work of tending Fred for the evening, then put on a soft light and showed Mitch the bathroom.

"Thank you. You're very kind to invite me to stay."

"You're always welcome, Mitch. I'll never be able to repay the debt I owe you, but I *can* provide a soft place for you to sleep."

"You don't owe me anything. It's my job."

She stared at him, waiting to pick up any of his thoughts. Evidently she was making a face while trying to do so, because he looked back at her with curiosity.

"What?" she demanded.

"What's going on? You're staring at me and you look like you're concentrating so hard you're about to blow a fuse or something."

"I can't hear what you're thinking."

He kicked off his shoes, smirking. "That's because I drank about a gallon of tequila on my own tonight, and I am not really having any thoughts." He turned down the covers and stood upright. "Good night, Kahrren."

She walked toward him with her hand out. He watched her hand move toward his shoulder. He didn't flinch or back away, so she made contact. She picked up a low groan from his mind, and then, *She's so pretty.*

She peered around him to the nightstand. "Do you need some wat—" The question was interrupted by a set of lips on her own. They were soft and warm, and completely unexpected. As far as kisses went, it was very nice, despite the understandable hesitation.

She kissed him back. She didn't even have to think about it. Her lips responded to him without consulting her brain. She felt his hand grasp her shoulders as the kiss deepened.

His thoughts became much, much clearer. She felt her body stir in response to the image in his mind of their bodies meeting. He slid his fingers into her hair as he devoured her mouth with his own. His body was as ready as hers was. She heard a soft, fearful plea float from his mind into hers. *Please don't say no. I need this.*

She gently pulled back from the kiss but didn't move to free her ass from his hand. "Are you sure?"

He let her go and stepped back. "I'll let you know if I change my mind." He pulled his shirt over his head and threw it on the chair adjacent to the bed.

Kahrren had imbibed an equal amount of tequila to what Mitch drank. *I can do this,* she thought. She grinned and moved across the room to close and lock the door.

* * *

Lorna sat across from Andrew at the kitchen table, sipping coffee while Andrew tried to convince his body to accept water in small sips. Kahrren looked like a wreck when she made it to the kitchen.

"Water. Must... have... water." She moved toward the cabinet, pulled out a glass, and filled it from the filtered water pitcher which resided next to the sink. Two full glasses disappeared before she set down her glass and picked up a mug to fill it with coffee.

"*So?*" Lorna was even perky when she was hung over.

"So, what?"

"I noticed you weren't on the couch this morning. Anything you'd like to talk about?"

"This coffee is extra strong today. Are you trying to punish me?"

"Andrew made it. Then he took a sip and set it down because he couldn't take it." She set down her cup. "But you know that's now what I meant."

"Do we have an extra toothbrush for our guest? I bet he'd like to brush his teeth."

"*Kahrren!*"

"Yes?"

"Out with it."

"Can you add some cocoa puffs to the grocery list? I think I'll go shopping today."

"You can't keep ignoring me, you know."

"Funny, I thought she was doing a pretty good job." Andrew stood up and moved toward the fridge. "Breakfast burritos?"

"Yes, please, dear, kind, handsome Andrew, who always minds his own business." Kahrren pulled her face upward in her best impression of a smile, but this was one hell of a hangover. Smiling did *not* come naturally.

"That sounds good, babe. Thank you." Lorna looked at Kahrren, and said, "Is he still here?"

"Well, did you think I was planning on delivering a new toothbrush to *his* house?"

"God, you're so rude. Also, you look frightful. You should go wash up before you scare the poor man."

"That one I'll agree with, Kahrren. Perhaps some ablutions are in order before our guest joins us." Andrew shrugged a shoulder. "Use our bathroom."

"Is it very bad?"

Her question was answered with dead silence.

"Uh-oh. I'll go." She made her way to the hallway and hit the shower. Not wanting to miss what Mitch would look like when he got up, she made short work of it and re-dressed at record speed. Before returning to the kitchen, she found the package of oral care products, and slipped into her bathroom as quietly as possible to leave a toothbrush for him. "He'll have to cope with my natural face because I am not putting on makeup today," she said as she returned.

Kahrren sat and casually sipped her coffee while Lorna stared at her, scowling and thinking as loudly as she was able, *Tell me. Tell me. Tell me.*

Andrew set a stack of plates on the table with one hand and a platter with breakfast burritos and quesadillas in the middle. As he returned with condiments, the floor outside Kahrren's room squeaked, and alerted them to Mitch's impending arrival.

A few seconds later, he walked in, freshly showered, and dressed in yesterday's clothing. "Smells great. I'm starving." He smiled and headed for the coffee maker. After pouring his cup, he joined the others at the table. "Good morning, everybody."

"Good morning." They all answered.

Lorna picked up some tongs and started placing food on everyone's plate.

"You're gonna make a great mother one day." Kahrren started to give an utterance of gratitude but as she started to speak, she saw a small but extraordinarily bright white light flash and momentarily emit a golden glow over Lorna's lower abdomen. She jumped up and out of her seat, backpedaling until she was against the wall behind her. She gasped and her hand flew over her mouth. "Lorna!"

"What?"

Kahrren's eyes lowered and stared in awe at the arrival of a new little soul.

Thank you, dear reader, for coming with me on this journey. If you enjoyed this book, please consider leaving a review on your favorite platform. As as independently published author, the small kindness is an invaluable asset.

Keep an eye out for the next part of the Psychic Touch Series early next year.

In Touch,
Kenna

Let's connect!

Website: www.kennacharlesauthor.com
Instagram: www.instagram.com/kennacharlesauthor
Facebook: www.facebook.com/kennacharlesauthor
Twitter: @KennaAuthor

Made in the USA
Las Vegas, NV
26 July 2023